"Readers will be captivated by the nonstop action in Mary Whitcombe. Nifora's story of a young, orphaned girl includes murder, deceit, greed, romance, love, and hope. The ultimate page-turner, readers will be stunned by what happens next and will be left wanting more."—Hannah Stutz, **Manhattan Book Review**

Mary Whitcombe

Other books by Valerie Nifora

I Asked the Wind: A Collection of Romantic Poetry

The Fairmounts (Book 1)

Unleash the Power of You: A Step-by-Step Guide to Creating and Sustaining Your Own Personal Brand

Mary Whitcombe

VALERIE NIFORA

AUTHOR ACADEMY elite

Identifiers:
Library of Congress Control Number: 2023918635
979-8-88583-268-7 (paperback)
979-8-88583-269-4 (hardback)
979-8-88583-270-0 (ebook)

Available in hardcover, softcover and e-book.

To Alan—
my North Star,
my always.

To love is to will the good of the other.
—St. Thomas Aquinas

Chapter 1

I remember very little of my childhood. I was so young when my world was torn apart. It hardly seems possible even now that I live and breathe.

I have a singular image in my mind of this woman laughing. The sound is warm and inviting. I love her smile; it brightens my heart. Her eyes are a lovely emerald green, and her dark hair is pulled up with little curls falling down the side of her face. She's wearing a green ribbon in her hair. I see it as the wind has blown off her hat. She is a Gibson Girl in my memory.

And there's a man. He has a kind face. I see him chasing after the hat, laughing. His voice is calm. "I'll catch that for you, Grace! The wind will not defeat me. I am above it all. I will fly like Hermes!" And he's off—in his brown trousers, suspenders and white button shirt with the sleeves rolled up to his elbows.

That is all I remember. That warm, sunny day with the wind blowing over the moors. And I can only suppose those were my parents, William and Grace Whitcombe.

It's the memory I've held on to so tightly and dreamed of so fiercely even to this day. It is my happy memory, the one I visit when all the world is falling apart. My grounding. I've always believed there was an "other" life I should be living, another life that escaped me because I was too little to grasp and hold it.

I have few memories of my house and my nursery. My bed was soft and filled with frilly things. The blankets had lace on the edges. There was a stuffed rag doll and a small stuffed rabbit made of velvet. These were my companions.

I remember lots of light flowing into the nursery and a lovely fountain outside the window. If I close my eyes, I can almost hear it trickling.

I have no memory of my nanny, whether she was kind or not, lenient or severe. I remember a rocking horse. I remember liking my rocking horse. It was near a small table with porcelain teacups. I must have had tea with my toys.

I think I was a happy child. I must have been. They say the first few years of a person's life determine her disposition, and I like to think I am happy, or I am capable of a condition that is referred to as "happy." But I have spent the majority of my life as a castaway, something no one wants, handed from one person to another person and finally to myself. And who am I really? What did I owe the world? Was it more likely the world owed me?

I remember his face when he came for me. He wore his glasses at the tip of his nose and had a soft voice. He was my father's friend. I would sit on his lap, and he would bounce me on his knee as I pretended to ride a horse in the races. Sometimes I would win. Sometimes not. He would do this as he and my father discussed things in my father's study.

I remember the study having lots of lights and books and smelling of smoked pipe—a sweet and sticky smell. And when the window was left open, it also smelled of gardenias. Sometimes I would take my doll and hide under my father's large mahogany desk. I remember it had carvings of little cherubs around the edges.

I don't remember that day being different from any other when that man came into my nursery. I must have been about four or five at the time. "Hello, Mary," he said.

"Hello," I responded. "Father's not here. He went away on a big ship, but I'm too little to go." It was not unusual for him to visit me and play. I didn't mind his visits.

He nodded. "Would it be all right, Mary, if I sit here and have some tea with you?"

I nodded and showed him where to sit. In retrospect, I don't know how he managed to sit in that tiny chair. Perhaps he only pretended to sit in the chair and crouched, as I've seen my husband, Harry, do with our girls. It's hard to say, really.

He cleared his throat. "Mary, I need to tell you something about your parents . . . "

"Would you like one lump of sugar or two?" I asked.

"Two, please."

"Milk?"

"Yes, please."

After fixing his imaginary tea, I watched him stir the cup with my tiny silver spoon.

Taking a deep breath, he said, "Mary, your parents . . . " A small tear fell down his face. "Mary, your father," another deep breath, "your mother." Full stop. A handkerchief emerged. "What I'm trying to say, Mary, is that your parents loved you very much. And they left specific instructions on how to care for you and your sister, should anything happen to them. And something has happened . . . I am to take you now."

"Take me where, Uncle Thomas?"

Another tear fell.

"I am supposed to take you home with me now. And then to someplace else."

"Uncle Thomas, I have a home, and I don't need to go someplace else. You're being very silly. Have some more tea."

I remember his hands trembling as he tried to hold the teacup.

Uncle Thomas didn't take me that day, but things were different in the house. It felt empty and quiet Uncle Thomas would come and go, and so would boxes. Large boxes of things on horse-drawn carriages I watched outside my window.

I ate mostly in my room. I saw few people. I'm sure one of them was my nanny. It was hard to tell with solemn faces. I didn't play in the gardens anymore.

I'm not sure I fully understood that my parents weren't returning. I think somewhere in my mind, I thought they were just gone for a while, and at some point, they would return. Death had little meaning for me then. It seemed an idea far too out of reach for me to comprehend.

I don't remember my sister; I understand she was a few years older than I was, but I have no memory of her young. For years, I assumed she went with my parents, far away on that big ship. Then, a lifetime later, I learned that was not true. She was very much alive, but that would come much later in my complicated tale.

I remember I would hear the church bells in the distance on Sundays. I hadn't been to church in what felt like years. Ever since my parents left on that big ship, no one cared to dress me and take me there.

It was a solitary life. I had my dolls and my window. I would look out my window for hours, just resting my head on my arm, looking out over the landscape of trees and small houses. I watched the seasons move from the warmth of the spring and summer to the sleepy mood of autumn. Out in the distance was the white steeple of the church. I could see it peeking from the leaves as they began to fall.

On this particular Sunday, I heard shouting. I ran and pressed my ear to the door.

"You can't leave the girls!" a shrill man's voice said.

"I can, sir, and I will. I have taken another position as a governess. With the Whitcombes

dead, sir, I can no longer stay here."

"But I pay you!" the man's voice said again. "The Whitcombes have left a fortune to care for the girls."

"Nevertheless, a living employer is better than a dead one. I will be leaving by week's end."

"Week's end! How am I to find a replacement by week's end? And with Fiona's condition. How in the world am I supposed to find someone in a week to care for that girl? You are absolutely in the wrong in this!"

"Nevertheless, sir, I have given you my notice," she said coldly.

"Who is going to care for the girls?" he insisted.

"There is a family with other children whom Mr. Whitcombe would visit. Perhaps them."

"I will not have the Wilkinses soil the girls' reputations! William was never serious!"

"You can care for them yourself."

"I am a bachelor! Are you mad? I don't know the first thing about raising girls!"

"Then send them to the convent." I could hear her retreating footsteps, followed by a large bang on the wall and sobbing, deep sobbing as if someone's soul were being ripped apart. I was too frightened to open the door.

"Blast you, William." He sobbed. "You leave me the impossible task of caring for your girls, and I am ill-equipped. Why did Grace go with you? You awful fool. Damn you both."

Backing away quietly from the door as if I had intruded into the most private of conversations, I found my way to my bed and, placing the covers over my head, fell asleep.

I don't know exactly what time it was when I awoke the next day, but I found a cup of milk, scrambled eggs, and some toast on the little table before me. At the washbasin, I cleaned my hands and face and settled my doll in the chair opposite me before sitting down to eat. Then there was a gentle rapping on the door. It opened, and there was Uncle Thomas. I was so delighted to see him that I ran and put my arms around his legs.

"I've hardly seen anyone since Papa and Mama left. I think there's a magic fairy that comes and leaves me food. Come sit with me, Uncle Thomas. Come sit and share my eggs." Leading him to the table, I had him sit and pushed my plate over to him, offering him a fork.

Again, a tear fell from his eye. "That is very kind of you, Mary. You have a good heart." And pushing the plate and fork back to me, he said, "I ate my breakfast. It's almost noon, and you'll need to eat yours."

Nodding, I began to eat the eggs. They were cold and a bit rubbery. "I think the cook forgot the salt," I whispered.

He laughed. "Mary, when you are finished. I'd like you to put on your very best dress. You can dress yourself, can't you?"

I nodded. "I still need help with the buttons."

"I'll find someone to help you with those. And then we're going to take a trip. I'd like you to pack all the things you love most. We're going to bring them with us."

"Where are we going?" I asked, eating my last bit of toast.

"Just over the hill and a little way. There are some women I'd like you to meet."

Nodding again, I finished my breakfast.

Chapter 2

I didn't realize it then, but I would not again return to my home as a child. It was the last time I would sleep in a warm and comfortable bed with lace and pillows of down feathers until I was a grown woman. Little sun would creep into my bedroom from then on. The warmth and comfort of wooden panels painted in a lovely shade of pink would be replaced by the gray stone of the drab universe in which I would live my next seventeen years.

If I had known, I would have looked at the house a bit longer. I would have hugged my pillow or packed it. I might have taken the soft blanket of silk and cashmere. I would have brought along my velvet rabbit. Thinking I would see him again, I left him in charge of the teacups and asked him to take care of them until my return. I only brought the rag doll my mother had made me.

The ride did not seem terribly long, but we passed through a small brook and a forest with trees that hung overhead and blocked the sun like an omen of what was to come. Uncle

Thomas held my hand in one of his and grasped a handker-chief in the other.

"It's a nice ride, isn't it, Mary?" he asked.

"I don't remember the carriage being so bouncy, but it is good to get outside. I haven't left my room, you know?"

At this, he seemed a bit startled. "What do you mean? You didn't go out, child?"

Shrugging, I said, "No one would come for me. Except for your visits, Uncle Thomas, I haven't played with anyone since Mama and Papa left."

I remember a look of shock and anger quickly flashing upon his face. He murmured, "Perhaps it's good she's leaving."

We started to ascend a steep hill, and the horses neighed at the weight of the carriage. "Easy!" the driver cautioned. "Almost there."

I could smell the soft scent of the ocean nearby. Almost immediately I heard the sound of hooves on cobblestone, and, releasing Uncle Thomas's hand, I kneeled on the seat trying to look out the window. The carriage made its way into a large courtyard. Before us was a gray stone building with a single story. It had a wooden door with nails and metal and a big brass knocker. There was a slight overhang that blocked the sun and small windows around the perimeter. If there was any cheer behind those walls, it was lost upon the façade of the building.

To the left of the building was a modest church. It was also made of stone and had a tall tower and a bell of dark metal. The windows of the church were in beautiful arches with colors that sparkled through. I thought of them as candy and wanted to run and touch them. The church and those beautiful windows would be the very first thing I ever painted.

Uncle Thomas opened the door and carried me out. Grabbing my hand, he took a deep breath and walked toward the door, but before he could grab the knocker, the door swung open. There stood five women in dark robes and funny white hats. I thought them beyond peculiar. Upon their robes, they wore massive crosses. The one who spoke had the largest cross; hers was speckled with stones.

"Welcome, Mr. Payne. And you must be Mary." I don't recall whether Mother Superior had joy in her tone or not. Perhaps it was just how I always remember it: strong, unemotional, matter- of-fact.

"Yes. Yes, this is the Mary Whitcombe of whom we spoke," Uncle Thomas offered.

"Hello!" a friendlier voice came from behind Mother Superior. This woman had a kind face. She was younger and cheerful, and she knelt before me and looked me in the eye. "I am Sister Ann. Is this your doll?"

Clinging to my doll, I said, "Yes. I call her Dollie, and I love her very much. Would you like to hold her?" I'm not sure why I gave Sister Ann my doll. Perhaps it was just her manner. She was a gentle, pleasant, talented soul who only saw the good in all things.

Mother's Superior's voice was stern. "Sister Ann, why not take the child—"

"Mary," Sister Ann corrected.

Undeterred, Mother Superior continued, "Why don't you take the child, *Mary*, to the garden and show her our flowers? Mr. Payne and I have a few things to discuss. This way, Mr. Payne."

Nodding, Sister Ann stood up and offered me her hand.

As gray and lifeless as the courtyard was, the garden was an entirely different world. There were roses and lavender and gardenias. There was a beautiful painted statue of the Virgin Mary in the center and small fountains on either side. Our feet crunched on the small stones and shells as we walked the path toward her.

"Are these shells?" I asked excitedly.

"Yes. They come from over there." Sister Ann pointed to where the hill began to slope down.

"Is it far? Can we go see it?" I asked excitedly. Motioning for me to sit next to her on the bench, Sister Ann said, "It's too far for today. Perhaps another time."

The sun was warm, and butterflies flew and landed on different flowers. There were colored birds that bathed in the fountain. This would serve as my special spot forevermore. If you go there now, you'll find my initials carved in the stone, "M. W." I don't know if Mother Superior ever noticed.

We sat there in silence for a while, and then Uncle Thomas found us. Holding his hat, he said, "Mary, I have to go now." And hopping off the stone bench, I offered my hand. "No, dear. You're going to stay here for a while with Sister . . . "

"Ann," Sister Ann said, smiling.

"Why?" I asked.

"Well, Mary, I think they'll be able to care for you now."

"For how long?" I asked.

"For a bit. Until . . . until things can be figured out. You don't mind staying with Sister Ann, do you, dear? It's beautiful here in the garden. And there are all these other sisters to care for you, play with you, read you stories, and help you grow up. Mary, I don't know how to do those things."

"But there aren't other children," I protested.

"I put your things in the room Mother Superior told me to put them in," he finished, looking up at Sister Ann for approval.

"No. Uncle Thomas, I'd like to go home now."

"This will be home for a while now, Mary," Uncle Thomas said firmly.

"No, it is not!" I stamped my foot. "I want to go back to my window and my bed and my bunny. He'll be very lonely watching my teacups!" And then I began to cry, my sobs so deep, I could not breathe.

"Mary. Mary, please. *Please.* I will bring you your bunny. I will be back with him tomorrow. Just stay one night with Sister Ann. Will you promise me you'll stay one night with Sister Ann, and we will talk tomorrow?" Hugging me tightly, he kissed my head, turned and ran toward the gate and into the carriage, slumping down and trembling.

Sister Ann scooped me up and held me. "*Shh . . .* " she said, "I promise to take good care of you, Mary. Forever, as long as I live, no harm will come to you. Nothing will happen to you."

Sniffling through gasps of air, I asked, "Will you be my mother now?"

And holding me even tighter, she promised, "Yes, if you so wish. I will be your mother now."

Chapter 3

Sister Ann did her best to settle me in the first night. I remember her walking me through the corridors and eventually to the room that would forevermore be mine and hers. If I close my eyes, I can hear the creaking of the heavy wooden door and the sound of the brass knob as she turned it.

I held my breath as she opened the door. And there it was—a small cell, my home from that moment forward.

The walls were of a gray stone that felt jagged when touched. On either side of this rectangular room were two small cots. There was a small wooden dresser between those beds and an oil lamp placed on top. Next to it was a series of old leather books, and at the foot of the bed I assumed to be Sister Ann's was a small slanted wooden table with a stool. And next to that, the one window in the entire room looked out onto a courtyard.

"Come, Mary," Sister Ann said. "This is where we will live now, and you'll never be alone." Holding my hand, she led me into the room with my doll tucked into her other arm. We walked a few steps, and, releasing my hand, Ann held up my rag doll. "Dollie! Look around! Isn't it grand? We have our own special room now!" Twirling around, she started to dance with my doll.

And as frightened as I was, I started to giggle. "Sister Ann, you're silly!"

"I can't hear you, Mary! Dollie and I are busy learning how to do a waltz!" She started to hum louder. "Oh, look how divinely she waltzes!" Sister Ann smiled and went round and round in circles.

I remember the tune she sang. It was the same one I heard when I would hide on the steps and peek into the grand ballroom where Mama and Papa held parties. I can picture them even now, dancing and smiling, a small fragment of my memories.

"Come, Mary! Join us!"

Before I could even protest, it was Dollie, Sister Ann and me, giggling and circling the little space we had in the room. This was Sister Ann's way. She always tried to take whatever fears I had and cast them aside by distracting me. She knew what I would fear before I knew I would fear it.

Finally, out of breath, Sister Ann sat down on her bed and handed me Dollie. I looked around the small room. I started to measure it with my steps – from the door to the dresser, from the bed to the bed. In time, I wandered over to her slanted desk.

"Sister Ann," I asked, "why is this table so strange?"

"Oh!" she exclaimed, smiling. "This is a drafting table! Let me show you." When she lifted the lid slightly, I saw colored pencils, papers, sketches, and a large black leather book that was held together by a small black leather strap. Seeing I was interested, she pulled a sketch and the book out and placed them on top of the angled table.

"I like to sit here on the stool by the window and draw. If you'd like, I can teach you."

When she invited me to look over her drawings, I saw in them the most beautiful gardens, birds, and butterflies. All her sketches were of the outdoors.

"I know this one! This is the fountain in the courtyard where we sat! It's quite good," I said nodding.

Ann smiled. "Yes. I rather like that one myself."

"Who is this man, Sister Ann?" It was the only person I saw in her drawings. It was a side view of a man who was sitting on a stool. His arms were at his side, his gaze downward as he held a book. He was handsome in a gentle way.

Ann took a deep breath before answering, "I think you should just call me Ann. This man was my husband. We weren't married very long before he died."

"Why in the world did he die?" I asked, very upset about the idea.

"He got very sick. We were married, and then a few months later, he died. I knew he was sick when I married him. But I did not care. He made me happy. All my life he made me happy."

"What was his name?"

"Matthew. His name was Matthew, and I knew him since I was smaller than you, Mary!"

"Will you tell me about him?" I was sitting on her bed now.

"I think I will tell you more about him another time." But seeing my disappointment and my reluctance to give her back the drawing, she sighed deeply and began, "My father did not want me to marry Matthew. He said I was going to steal him from God. Matthew always loved the church and the scriptures, and I think he would have been a fine priest. But the world had other plans. We fell in love. We got married. He got very sick. He died, and I decided I would dedicate my life to God in his place, for giving us those few months of happiness together. You know you love someone, Mary, when thinking about them, even though they are gone, still makes you happy." I did not know this at the time, but no words rang truer in my life than these.

I did not understand what that all meant, so I handed her the picture and decided not to ask any more about him. I did not want to make Ann sad.

"Ann, I would very much like you to teach me how to draw," I said after silence had fallen between us. "I used to draw with Uncle Thomas, but he never drew anything as good as you. I want to draw like you do. I very much like your flowers and birds." Ann looked down at her sketch. Solemn.

I took a small step closer to her. "I'm sorry about Matthew."

"I am sorry about Matthew too. I always thought that if God saw fit to let him live longer, we might have had a little girl. I always loved the name Mary." Here she winked at me and smiled. "I would very much love to teach you how to draw. It would give me great joy, if you'd like to learn it. I don't share this to many people," she leaned in closely, "but before I married Matthew, I went to art school. It is unheard of for girls to do that, you know." And here, she winked again.

"How did you manage to do that?" I asked, astonished.

"Another time, Mary. When you are older."

We ate in our rooms that night, sitting on the floor. Ann had the other sisters bring our dinner on two trays. It was a humble meal of fresh bread and bean soup. Not at all like the pheasants, fruit and puddings I would have in my home. But it filled me, and I was happy to eat.

As the evening closed around us, Ann asked the sisters to find me a small trunk to place at the foot of my bed. We unpacked my few things and stored them in there. Taking a pillowcase from her dresser, she made a bed for my doll to sleep in, then placed her on the trunk. Tucking her in, we said our prayers. I remember her being so pleased that I knew them.

She sat on the floor that night, holding my hand until I fell asleep. She held my hand so many times throughout the years, always whispering, "Remember, Mary, you are not alone, and I will always be here." Ann kept her promise until I was grown.

Chapter 4

Mother Superior secured an appropriate education for me while I was in her care. As the years went by, I became quite versed in many subjects. In addition to Ann's art, I was able to learn French, mathematics, European history, gardening, sewing, and archery. Mother Superior wanted to ensure that if I chose not to stay at the convent when I came of age, I could, at the very least, employ myself as a governess.

Although archery might seem out of place, Sister Francis had been a world class toxophilite before joining the order. These were extraordinary women who lived in the convent, each with their own path and story that found them here behind these walls. And for most of it, we were happy.

The convent managed to sustain itself through candle-making with beeswax procured by the bees we kept. We also sold honey and propolis to help with various ailments. We had a small garden that we tended and sold whatever excess we could in the market. Every so often, someone from the nearby village with a severe illness would come and ask for Sister Maxine to cure them, for she was known for her skills with apothecary. This was often to the dismay of the local physician. I always wondered if it was the prayers for healing or her concoctions that cured the ill.

My childhood years passed very quickly and, before I knew it, I was on equal footing with the sisters. I was most certainly as tall as Sister Ann, and I no longer looked like a child. I was not thought of as a child any longer, but as a young woman, a member of their family. Although I didn't wear a full habit, I would still partake in the ceremonies and celebrations. I would sing in the choir and have my appointed chores and responsibilities. In time, any sadness I felt as a child became replaced with the predictability of each day. This gave me great comfort.

I distinctly remember the day that would change my life forever, the extraordinary disruption of the ordinary. I was running between my appointed classes from French to mathematics. They were scheduled at opposite sides of the dormitory, which was Mother Superior's intent, to ensure I received the proper amount of physical movement during the day and eliminate any effects of lethargy.

It was such a lovely day. The harsh winter had given way to the warm ocean breezes. I closed my eyes and let the warm sun fall on my face. The church bell marking the time signaled that I had dawdled too long, and Sister Maxine would not be pleased. I decided to attempt to save myself the admonishment from my mathematics teacher and take a shortcut across the courtyard with the fountain, a direction I often avoided as it always reminded me of Uncle Thomas and the last time I saw him when he left me behind.

And there he was: a young man poised on a ladder leaning over the large fountain in the middle of the rose garden. His dark curly hair protruded from his woven straw hat with his sleeves rolled up to his elbows, stains on his linen shirt, and light blue suspenders. He was a most unexpected sight. He might not have taken any notice of me if not for my surprise and haste, causing me to fall face first into the shells and gravel.

"*Giovane donna*!" he yelled in a language I had not heard before as he came down the ladder in a rush. "*Stai bene*? Are you alright?" he asked again with a heavy intonation to each word. After helping me sit up, he crouched beside me and brushed the small shells and pebbles from my hair. His nimble fingers were brown and stained with dirt.

The bell had marked its last trill. I was mostly certainly late.

"How did you fall?" His words sounded peculiar to me. It was clearly foreign with heavy consonants and nothing like French.

Looking at him closely now, I could see that, beneath his dark, unruly curls that hung around his complexion, were his warm eyes in the most beautiful shade of blue I had ever seen. He smiled gently and said, "You are alright," nodding in his own agreement. "But you have cut your face a little." Reaching into his pocket, he pulled out a handkerchief and started to press it on my face. "Here. It is but a small thing. It will not scar your beautiful face."

By now, Sister Maxine had wandered out to find me, and seeing me on the ground with the young man inspired her to quicken her step and run toward us. "What happened? Goodness, Mary! Are you alright?"

The young man smiled again. "Mary. That is a good name. Like the Virgin Mother. *La Vergine Maria*."

My face must have turned several shades of crimson. "I fell."

"The young lady was running, and she fell down. Right here. I was up there." Turning, he pointed to the ladder leaning against the fountain. "I saw her go down. She will only have a small cut on her face. She will have no scars and will still be beautiful tomorrow."

"Who are you?" Sister Maxine inquired, slightly perturbed.

"Oh. Yes. *Mi scusi*, I am Marco. I am the new gardener." And, after wiping his hand on his pants, he extended it to Sister Maxine, who was both bewildered and confused.

Sister Maxine stared at Marco intently as she lifted me up to stand. "You must be mistaken. We don't have men stay here. Come, Mary." Expecting me to follow along, she turned away, only to find me back on the ground behind her.

"I can't walk!" I said in a bit of a panic.

"No. Don't worry. You must have twisted your leg. You will be alright. It was not a big fall. I will run and get Mother Superior." After saying such, he ran to the grand entrance, and, within minutes, he returned with Mother Superior.

"Let's see it, Mary." Mother Superior bent down, touching my right ankle, which had begun to swell now. Taking a deep breath, she concluded, "Well, it seems you'll be taking the mathematics classes in your room. Sister Maxine, go bring me some cloth, and we'll bind Mary's ankle."

"Who is that man?" was the only thing Sister Maxine could say.

"Who does it look like? The gardener. Oh, never mind." Lifting me up to my legs again, she put my arm around her shoulder and had me hobble back into the main building, leaving a stunned Sister Maxine and concerned Marco out in the courtyard. Then she called out, "Sister Maxine, if you can manage to lift your jaw from the ground, I could use your help with Mary."

Mother Superior brought me to her office, placing me in a wooden chair by the door. She removed my shoe and stocking. Pressing on my ankle gently, she concluded that the bone was intact. It was decreed that the swelling would subside in time, with Sister Maxine concurring.

It was Marco who interrupted their banter, "*Mi scusi*," he said again, "but I bring this to help Mary." He held in his hand a large branch with a limb in the form of a V. After placing it under my arm, he helped me stand and then asked me to use it to support my weight.

"I bring you to your room, all right? You show me where to go." He smiled.

"I'm not sure you should be wandering about the corridors here, Marco," Mother Superior said sternly.

"I won't wander, Mother Superior. I only help Mary."

Almost as if by the Divine, the bell tower rang again. Knowing she would be late to prayers, Mother Superior grunted her approval and rushed to the chapel with Sister Maxine scurrying after her, black robes flowing.

"I will show you how to use this. We will do it slowly. You can lean on me. You show me how we go back to where you stay." He smiled again, and, holding me up, we slowly started to move. Unlike the sisters, who smelled of incense and honey, Marco smelled of roses, lavender and earth. I found him intoxicating.

"My mother, when I was a small boy, she made me something like this to help. I used to fall down all the time. I was too busy looking at the flowers to know where I was going." And he laughed. "I love flowers. They are my whole life."

I'm not sure, but I believe this was the moment I fell in love with Marco. But how can anyone be sure of anything when she is fourteen years of age?

We managed slowly step by step through the courtyard and off to the section of the dormitory where Sister Ann and I lived. As we went, Marco would encourage me, laughing and smiling. I could feel his strong arms help prop me up.

If I close my eyes, I can still feel his breath on my shoulders as he walked with me, helping me learn how to manage this massive walking stick with a V that he had placed under my arm. I didn't have the heart to tell him that it hurt my arm to keep trying to move along with it. He seemed so happy to help.

The massive bang of the door swinging open to our cell startled Ann, forcing her to involuntarily stand in haste and drop her Bible. "God bless!" she exhaled; her eyes wide. She looked confused as to who this man was and why he was carrying me into my room.

Gently, he scooped me up and placed me on my bed, smiling down at me. Turning to Ann, he extended his hand. "I am Marco. I am the new gardener."

Ann shook his hand, and, after taking a moment to find her own voice, she swallowed hard, and said, "I am Sister Ann. I am Mary's mother. I mean, I look after Mary."

"I see. It is a pleasure to meet with you, Sister Ann." He smiled and giggled.

"What happened?" Ann asked, looking at me.

"I was running to get to mathematics and fell on the shells. I hurt my ankle, but Mother Superior and Sister Maxine thinks it will heal."

"It must have been the sun. It maybe got into her eyes, and she was confused, so she fell. It used to happen to me as a boy. You have to be careful of Apollo." Looking at both of us, he concluded, "I have to go back to fixing the fountain. You be careful. You will heal." He clasped his hands together and, bowing slightly, left the room.

"Why aren't you in prayers?" I asked.

"I wasn't feeling all that well, and Mother Superior excused me." She lifted the Bible off the floor, kissed it, and placed it on her bed.

"Is it the headaches again?" I asked.

Ann nodded, and, lying down on her bed, she closed her eyes. "I'm glad it was nothing more serious, Mary. But I don't think it was the sun that blinded you."

We both giggled. I closed my eyes to pray silently with Ann, but instead, sleep overtook me.

The warmth of the day and the breeze that came through the window lulled me into tranquility, helping me forget the pain in my ankle. It was the muffled sounds through the door hours later that stirred me. I strained to hear what they were saying.

"How in the world do we have a male gardener?" It was Ann who spoke.

"It is a favor to the bishop. It's his nephew," Mother Superior responded.

"You know full well that we can't have a young man staying with us in the convent." Ann was quite stern. "Especially with a young girl like Mary about."

"Sister Ann, he is staying in the loft above the bell tower, tucked far away from any of us. He will only be with us from spring through summer and then return back to Rome in the fall. Mary is your responsibility. I'm sure you'll keep her occupied with her studies. As I mentioned, he is here as a favor requested of me by the bishop, and I cannot tell the bishop no, can I?" Mother Superior sounded quite emphatic on that point.

"What in the world did the boy do to have him cast off in the English countryside?" Ann asked incredulously.

"I sincerely don't care," was Mother Superior's response, and then I heard heavy-laden footsteps walking down the corridor and away from my door.

"Margaret! You know full well this is a mistake, especially for Mary!" Ann shouted after her. There was no reply.

For the next few weeks, I did not see Marco. My instructors came to me. Meals were delivered to my room. Marco vanished from conversation and consideration as quickly as he had come, and I wondered if perhaps I had imagined him out of some loneliness. A reasonable explanation if it were not for the tall walking stick he had crudely crafted for me, which stood leaning behind the door.

It was on a particular afternoon; I heard a gentle, unexpected rapping on the door. It was out of place, as it was not time for instruction or meals. I stared curiously as the door slowly creaked open. Marco peeked his head inside my room. He wore his same dirt-stained shirt and light blue suspenders with one sliding down his left shoulder. Smiling, waiting for permission to enter my room, he presented me with a rose through the crack in the door.

"I wanted to see how you were. It's been many weeks since you fell, and the sisters just told me that everything is alright, but you know, I wanted to see for myself. I can come inside?" With this last question, his eyebrows arched a little. "I bring a gift this time, better than your stick."

I smiled and nodded.

He cautiously crept into my room as if expecting land mines with each foot fall. Looking steadily around, he found my glass of water on the trunk in front of my bed and placed the rose there. It was a light pink color with darker pink around the edges. I had never seen anything quite like it in my life.

"You like it?" he asked. "I brought it over from Italy when I come with my uncle the bishop."

"Your uncle is the bishop?" I asked incredulously and motioned for him to sit on the edge of my bed.

"Yes. He takes a tour from Rome in the spring and summer, and he is meeting with people here and there. I don't want to go along, so he said I can stay here and tend to the flowers and fix the fountain. I think I'm going to build another rose garden in the courtyard there." He pointed to the space outside Ann's window. "There are no roses there. I study space. I was hoping I would see you, but I only see your Sister Ann." He gestured to the book I held in my hand. What do you read?"

I stared at him, fascinated. Up until this point, I had grown up with women. I saw men in the comings and goings of townfolks, clergy or the infirmed, but Marco was something entirely different.

"History." I showed him the book.

"Ah! Yes. I read this in school too. It is nice that the sisters give you books to learn."

"How old are you?" I asked.

He smiled again. "I am seventeen. I will be a year older in two weeks, and if you can walk by then, you will have to come and see my flowers. Until then, I will be outside the window, working in the dirt."

I nodded. "You are older than me."

Smiling, he stood up. "You look for me there." He pointed to the window by Ann's bed, in the empty space in the courtyard. Closing the door behind him, he left my room.

Chapter 5

True to his word, Marco started the next morning in the courtyard, much to Ann's displeasure. She woke up screaming and then drew the curtains closed. Each morning when she left for her morning chores, I would sit on her bed and pull the curtains back slightly so I could see Marco. He would whistle while he dug in the hard earth, and on rare occasions, he would hum. He would pretend he did not know I was watching him work, but he knew I was there. Sometimes, he would look at the drawn curtains and wink.

He kept track of time by the shadows the sun would cast, and when it was time for my instructions, he would pick up his shovel and go elsewhere so he was never a distraction to my learning. In the two weeks' time, he removed all the brambles, made the dirt smooth, and started to plant flowers. I, for my part, was able to walk more comfortably.

It was on his birthday that I found him outside by the gates as I walked past the infamous fountain that had caused my debacle. He leaned against the stone wall waiting for me with a lunch pail in his hands.

"I see you walk better!" he called out.

"Yes. I can walk now. Thank you. Whom are you waiting for?"

"For you, of course, *bella giovane signora*!"

"I don't know what that means."

"It means 'beautiful young lady' in my language. You are going to take a walk with me down to the water after that hill, and we are going to have a lunch. I have the food I put into this pail, and we will celebrate your foot being better and me being eighteen years old today. You can walk, yes?" he asked full of confidence, then added quickly, "If you have any trouble, I will carry you. You were light as a feather."

And so, we walked quietly down the hill to the water. I had walked there many times before with Ann and by myself. It was a familiar path to me, as I did so love the water and the sound of the waves crashing along the shore. But on that day, it was different. I had no chaperone. I had no experience with a boy near my age. I had no expectations or ideas at all.

I knew but one thing, which was that I enjoyed the feeling I had when I was near Marco, but I couldn't place what it was. It was so different than any other feeling I had up until that point in my life. He would make my heart flutter. I would wait to hear his voice. I would imagine his voice when whatever I was studying could not hold my attention. I looked forward to seeing his face and getting lost staring into his eyes, and there was something extraordinarily captivating about his smile.

When we reached the beach, Marco unbuttoned his shirt and placed it down on the sand so I might have a place to sit. I remember an uncomfortable excitement that I tried hard to squelch.

"I don't want you to get your dress dirty," he said nonchalantly as if was the most ordinary thing to do. Perhaps it was in his world. After sitting down on the sand himself, he handed me some bread and cheese and then turned to stare at the sea. We sat there quietly for a while, eating and listening to the tide roll in.

"Mary, I have to leave in a few weeks as the summer will be over, and I wanted to tell you that I am grateful for the time we spent together, even if it was through the window. You were a nice reminder of my friends and family back home. I hope, Mary, I can say that you are my friend." Here, he turned and looked at me with his beautiful blue eyes.

"Yes. Of course. Why shouldn't we be friends?" I asked.

He seemed pleased. "It was nice to have another young person here. The island where my mother is from, the water is a beautiful blue and calm. I am surprised how dark and disturbing the water is here. It has a different, dark power here."

"What island is that?"

"The village is called Positano. It's in Italy. I have cousins there. I have a lot of family everywhere."

"I don't have family anywhere," I said solemnly. "My parents and sister died when I was very small, and that's how I came to live here among the sisters. I suppose they are my family now."

He sat quietly, considering how this was at all possible. "Mary, there is going to be a good life for you somewhere, because I feel it, and because we are friends. As you grow up, you will come to visit me, and we will be more family for you outside of the sisters."

And this brought great comfort to my heart.

As August wound down, Marco began to pack his things. The flowers had all bloomed, the sun was setting earlier, and there was a coldness that started to hang in the air.

I remember the day the bishop came and picked him up, and I watched him go away in his carriage. He waved at me through the window. I stood there watching as all the others went back into the church or dormitory. I stood there holding my elbows with my arms folded over my waist as the carriage got smaller and smaller and then disappeared.

I started to weep. Uncontrollable sadness gripped my heart, and I sat down hard on the ground. This was my first friend I'd lost, and I did not know if he'd ever come back. It was then that I realized heartbreak can take many forms.

It was Christmas when Ann dropped a letter on my bed. It had strange writing and strange postage. I had never in my life received a letter before. Who was there alive to write me? I sat on the edge of my bed studying it, trying to see how it would open. I unfolded the parchment and my heart leaped. It was a letter to me from Marco!

"Ann! Marco wrote me! We *are* friends!" I exclaimed and greedily devoured every word that was penned with a dark blue ink. I even smelled the paper to see if there was any hint of roses, lavender or earth.

He told me that he was well. That his family was well. That his sister was to marry soon, and he was excited. They were going to be married in a beautiful church in his village. He told me he was considering studying again. He wasn't sure, but there was a university known for horticulture where he would attempt to matriculate. And then he told me the thing that made my heart leap again. He said that he would be back in the spring.

I lit an extra candle at the service that evening. I asked for Marco's safe return to the convent and to me.

This is how it was for me and Marco. For three years, I'd see him come and work the gardens in the summer, and we'd write each other letters when we were apart. I kept them bound in a little wooden box with the pink satin ribbon I wore when I first came to the convent.

It was the early spring of my seventeenth birthday when he wrote me this letter, and it broke my heart.

My Mary,

I write to tell you that I am to be married to a beautiful girl, Christina. I am of the age for these things. I will come one last time through the summer and raise the roses for you. Be happy for me. I am happy. I will tell you more when I see you.

Marco

I was inconsolable. Not that I fancied I would marry Marco myself. I didn't really consider it. I also didn't expect anyone to be married to him either. I did not want this to be his last trip to the convent. I wanted him to come forever. That is how I had fashioned it into my mind: Marco would come every year, until we both grew too old to walk. This seemed too cruel and unfair a fate that he would come only once more. And then, forevermore, he would be gone, and I would be alone with nothing and no one to call my own.

I counted the days until I knew he would arrive. Every day I looked toward the gate, hoping a carriage would come and bring him. What if he married Christina early? What if she did not want him to come?

Did Christina even know of me? I would venture that she did not. And what was there really to know? What would he say exactly? He had some foolish young friend in England who looked forward to his visits and whose heart would soar when he walked into a room. How would that even be known to him?

How could he ever know that my heart would beat faster, and my skin would feel warmer, and my mind would absorb every single word he said and repeat it to comfort me when he was not nearby? How would he even know how hungrily I waited for each letter and that each word filled my soul until the time I would be able to see him again?

The day finally arrived when the carriage was due. Ann knew and excused me from my studies that day. I sat on the bench by the fountain as I had done as a little girl when I first came to the convent.

For the first time in my entire life, the convent and its surroundings felt small to me. I looked down the road which bent into trees, to see where the carriage would come. For the first time, I wondered what was out there beyond the gate? What would I find in the world, and what would the world find in me?

I never before thought about leaving the confines of the convent. I never had any desire. It was safe here and happy and full of people who cared for me. And yet, there was a restlessness now in my soul that could not be managed with morning prayers or hymns of praise.

It was warm again. I lay down on the bench, placing my arms under my head. I started to drift away. And there was the sound—a grinding and scraping of earth.

I sat up and placed my hand over my forehead to block the sun. I stared at the bend in the road with anticipation. It had to be his carriage approaching. No one else was due to come to the convent.

In what felt like an eternity, I finally saw it—two horses pulling the Hansom carriage. I could hear the bells ring. Standing up, I stared intently. Was Marco in there?

And then, I saw him. He leaned out the window, and with half his torso through the opening, he waved and yelled, "I have come back, my Mary!"

I could not help but bite my lip and smile. I cupped my hands around my mouth and yelled back, "I am so pleased you could!" And then I waved wildly.

With renewed spirit, the horses entered the courtyard, and when finally halted, they breathed heavily. I stood by the entrance now waiting to see Marco disembark first. I was still biting my lower lip in an awkward smile when the coach door opened and the coachman brought down the stairs, but this time, it was the bishop who departed first.

Immediately, a sense of shame washed over me at my frivolous response that the bishop heard. Falling to my knees, I bowed my head and placed my hands in prayer. I knew not to speak until the bishop spoke, and so I kneeled there in silence. How quickly my jovial heart had turned to penitence. I had only seen him once, many years ago. All the other times, the carriage had deposited Marco without him.

I was steadfast in staring at the rocks before me as I knelt. But another shadow approached, and this was a familiar voice.

"Uncle, this is my Mary, the friend I told you about who kept me company all those years here." He sounded too informal. This was the bishop.

"You can rise, child," the bishop said in a warm tone, placing his hand on my shoulder, and I did as told. I had never seen him this close before. He had a gentle face and the same beautiful blue eyes Marco had.

"The sisters do not expect me. I know, in years past, Marco would come alone, but I urgently need to speak to Mother Superior. Will you go and let her know I am here?"

I nodded. In awe, I could not utter a word and ran into the rectory to find Mother Superior. We both returned quickly.

After their proper greetings, they were off to discuss whatever it was the bishop found so important.

I followed them until they disappeared through the doorway. "Mary!" It was Marco's voice that broke me of my trance. "It's okay. He's only the bishop." And then he laughed in his usual way. "Come. Help me carry a few things back to the bell tower. I have something for you."

"Yes. Yes. Of course," I said. "I always help you with your things."

"Yes. It brings me luck for the season," he said.

There were sixty steps to the top of the bell tower that wound around in a circle and ended at a lovely stone archway and a stone bench designed to be part of the wall. Just beyond this construction was the wooden platform that served as the ceiling for the church below. And above the flooring hung the bronze bell with a large, thick rope. Marco always had to hold the rope by two hands to ring it. Past the platform and the bell, there was a large wooden door, and it was there in that cell that Marco would spend his time, tucked away from all the business of the convent and far away from all of us.

No one would venture into the chamber when Marco was away. It was always exactly at he had left it. Opening it slowly and clearing the cobwebs, Marco entered the room and made his way to the shutters to open them.

The light flooded the room. There was a wooden bed to the far wall with a dresser. It was always stripped bare when he left, and I would always make it for him when he returned, taking the bed linens from the drawers that were filled with lavender to avoid moths in the fall. Marco always stared out the windows while I did this with his bags on the floor by his side. Today was no different.

"I cannot believe this will be the last summer I will look out and see these views," he said with his hands on his hips.

The land stretched out before the content in a canopy of trees. To the right, if one were to look steadily, beyond the stone wall, was a small grassy hill that gently descended to the sandy beach and ocean.

Having completed my task, I sat on the edge of the bed looking at his silhouette cast a shadow on the floor. "I really don't want to think on that, Marco." I placed my hands in my lap.

He nodded and clasped his hands together. "We have an unusual freedom here. No other place, Mary, would you and I be left alone in a room for all these years. I want you to know, I will always cherish our friendship." He reached into a bag and pulled out a blue satin bag with a purple ribbon. Sitting next to me, he handed it to me. "This is for all those years, Mary."

Opening the bag slowly, I found a beautiful medallion on a silver chain. I did not know what to say.

"It is the Virgin Mother. For you, Mary. Your saint for you." He placed it around my neck as I lifted my hair and secured the clasp.

I can only imagine I beamed.

My hand reached up, and, with my tears filling my eyes, I could not say anything at all. It was beautiful.

It was Ann who entered next. "There you are!" she said, short of breath. "The stairs get harder each year."

"Look!" I said, rushing over. "Look what Marco gave me."

I couldn't place the look that passed across Ann's face before she said, "It's lovely."

"St. Mary for Mary," Marco said, placing his hands in his pockets. "This way, although I will not be here next year, Mary will always have me near."

"It's very thoughtful and expensive," Ann said. "You are both wanted in the hall, order of the bishop and Mother

Superior, for prayer service, but if you don't mind, I'd like to sit for a bit before we all go back down the steps. You don't need to wait for me to catch my breath, just let them know I will be along shortly."

I never really noticed that Ann was having more and more difficulty with steps. The pain in her head had increased more frequently, and even Sister Maxine's potions would not help for long.

Marco nodded in agreement, and he held my hand like we did when we were younger, as I followed him down the winding steps to the church. We each took our pews and kneeled. There was an unusual look on the bishop's face I could not place as we came down the aisle, almost one of pity or sorrow. Looking down at the floor, he took a deep breath, studied the pages in the book he held in his hands and continued on with the prayers.

The summer progressed like all the others before with the only exception being the extraordinary heat and the heaviness in my heart. For I knew that every moment would be my last with Marco. I desperately tried to memorize it all, so that when Marco left, I could relive the memories in the solitude of my own thoughts.

Marco seemed unfazed by the upcoming conclusion of our little arrangement. He worked in the garden, tended the flowers and hummed and whistled as if all was well. I was not well. I was not suited to change. Change had often forced my life in a direction not of my choosing.

But on this particularly hot day in August, Marco came knocking on my bedroom door. I was absorbed in my sketches with charcoal, trying to remember the exact arc of Marco's nose.

"Perfect!" I said as he opened the door. "You stand right there by the light, and I want you to look out the window so I can get the perfect angle."

Marco, looking amused, did as he was asked.

"Stay still!" I instructed sternly as I sat on my bed. "What brings you here to my room?"

"You mean, besides fate and heat?" He smiled. "What are you drawing?"

"It was you. Well, now that you moved, it's all over." I closed the book and placed it on my bed.

He laughed. "It's hot. Let's go swim."

I considered it.

"Fine, but I have to be back for vespers."

Marco nodded and made a cross over his heart. Now in agreement, we left and headed down to the shore.

The air felt thick. It took even longer than usual to reach the water. I regretted forgetting my hat as the sun beat down on us both. I remember stopping halfway there to reconsider.

"It *is* very hot today, Marco. Maybe we're better off in the shade. Maybe we should just go back and sit under a tree. We can swim tomorrow."

"We are almost there, my Mary. Look. We can hear the waves and see the tops of the arcs."

I took a step and hesitated. There was a strange pull propelling me back toward the convent. My fingers, unknown to me, had found the medallion around my neck and were rubbing it. We had traveled halfway now. It was the same distance to the water as it was to the convent. The perfect middle ground between what was and what was to be.

"Mary," Marco said sternly, "the water is *right there*." Turning, he pointed to it impatiently. Annoyed now at my hesitation, he started to walk toward it on his own and shouted back. "It is hot today!"

Reluctantly, I followed, the soles of my feet burning on the scorching sand. When we arrived at the shore, the waves were unusually strong. The sea looked angry—an awful green anger. I thought of what Marco said when he first saw the beach. He said that Poseidon was angry here. I would have shouted another plea to swim tomorrow, but Marco was so determined, he did not care. Running in the water without any regard, he dove into the first large wave and was lost to sight.

"Wait!" I yelled, fumbling with the buttons on my blouse. "Marco! Wait for me." Searching the waves, I could not see him. A mild panic gripped me as I tried to remove my blouse and skirt. I looked for any sign of Marco in the waves. He was a far superior swimmer than I was, and I could not fathom that he could be lost to the sea.

Where *was* he? Did the ocean really take him? Was he truly lost to me forever?

As the tears started to well in my eyes, and my hands tremble at the thought, *There!* A small dark tuft of hair emerged from the next large wave. Was that Marco? With the tuft came a broad smile and a wave. I released my breath relieved as Marco came back to the shore and, dripping wet, stood next to me.

"I am sorry, Mary. It is just too hot today. I feel like I am stuck in an inferno."

I smiled weakly.

"Come!" He grabbed my hand and led me to the water. "Stay close," he instructed. "Poseidon is angry today." He winked at me. I smiled that he remembered.

Feeling like Lazarus begging for just a drop of water in the afterlife, I too could not wait to feel a cool relief of the waves under throbbing feet. I stopped at the edge of the shoreline. One last moment to heed the warning in my soul, "Marco,

I think the bottom of my feet have blisters. We should wait until tomorrow."

"What is this with 'tomorrow'? Stay close to me. You will be fine," he said offhandedly, staring at the waves.

I was not sure. "The waves look harsh."

"Remember when we would swim to make your leg strong when you fell by the fountain so many years ago? I would hold your hand when you were afraid. Come. It is Hades out here. Come with me. Hold my hand."

I held his hand tightly as the water came to my waist. I had no desire to go any farther. Again, I felt an overwhelming urge to leave the water immediately and return to the convent in haste. Sensing I had now become a planted marble statue, Marco let go of my hand.

"Ah! You worry too much bella donna!" He was just a few feet before me, smiling and floating in the water when I saw it come.

It was as if a Cetus opened its massive mouth and inhaled. The waters receded. I lost my footing. A massive suction pulled me down to the bottom of the seabed. My arms and legs crashed hard against the rocks. I was disoriented.

I tried to remember what Marco taught me and looked for light. I held my breath and tried to calm my beating heart. "You'll be alright," I told myself. "You'll be alright. Stay calm."

I swam up toward the light, managed to break through to the surface and took a deep breath. I tried to yell for Marco, but down again I came. Down onto the rocks, out farther to the sea. I tried desperately not to despair. My lungs urged me to breathe. Breathe! They commanded. But I could not. I would not. And up again I rose. I gasped for air.

I was bracing myself for the battery I expected to come from the seabed when an arm reached down, grabbed my hand, and pulled me up. His arm was now under my torso and shoulders as he told me to keep my head above the water and keep breathing.

"We'll make it, Mary. We'll make it!" I heard a familiar voice. I closed my eyes, exhausted.

"Kick, Mary! Kick, Mary, and help me get you to the land," Marco yelled.

But I was too tired. I was so exhausted. I coughed. Water had come into my lungs. It was too hard. This was all too hard. But the safety of Marco's arms continued to soothe me. After lifting me out of the water and running onto the sand, Marco cradled me as he gently placed me down. "Breathe, Mary!" he commanded. He turned me onto my side and pounded my back, I coughed out water. Sitting upright, startled, I began to breathe.

I looked at my savior. His eyes were full of tears, and cradling me again in his arms, he started to rock me back and forth like one would an infant.

"You were right, Mary. We should not have come," he whispered into my hair. "My Mary." Releasing me gently, he searched my face. Slowly leaning down, he kissed me. It was the gentlest kiss. And, stroking my hair again, he said, "I'm sorry."

He lifted me up off the sand and held me like a child. With my arms around his neck, he began to walk slowly back to the convent. It was then that I realized I had lost my medallion. I no longer felt it around my neck. It was my sacrifice to Poseidon for allowing us both to live.

I don't know if it was my delay in returning for vespers, but we found the sisters assembled waiting for us in the courtyard. It was Sister Ann who reached me first and, stroking my hair, she began to cry. "Mary, oh thank God Mary."

"She almost drowned," was all Marco could whisper.

The doctor was called, and I was instructed to stay in bed for a few days to recover. Apparently, I was fortunate as two others were found drowned by the shore not far from us.

The doctor declared that Marco was nothing short of hero for saving me. He called him my guardian angel. He shook his hand when he departed and patted him on the back, saying, "Good fellow."

But Marco knew it was his insistence we swim that almost ended my life. He didn't feel the hero. He felt overwhelmingly guilty.

The next few days were filled with thunderstorms and uncharacteristic cold winds. As if the gods were angry their sacrifice was rescued. Each time I closed my eyes, I could not help but think of Marco's kiss. I played it over in my mind. I imagined how he smelled from the ocean. The softness of his lips. His beautiful tear-soaked eyes.

I had never been kissed before. It brought forth such an unusual madness. And in my jubilation, my mind would then wander to Marco leaving, and an all-absorbing jealousy would begin. He would no longer be mine. He would belong to another. I would be alone, and the weight of that overwhelmed me and cast a wicked shadow over my heart.

When the storms passed, and I was allowed to wander about, everything resumed as it was. Marco never mentioned the kiss or behaved affectionately toward me. If anything, he was more careful with me as if I were the most fragile thing alive.

We did not swim again. We avoided the beach. Neither would bring it up as a suggestion to the other. We spent the remainder of our summer under the shade of the trees, walks in the surrounding forest, and tending to flowers.

I know Marco was aware I lost my medallion in the waves that day, but he did not ask me about it, nor did I tell him. It was as if that entire experience was to be erased from our history. I locked it up in my heart to retrieve in lonely moments and relive as I saw fit.

When the time came for him to depart, he cut me a single rose from the garden, kissed my forehead and whispered in my ear, "You will always be my Mary."

Chapter 6

Christmas came, and I did not receive a letter or a greeting from Marco. I wrote to him to inquire about his wedding preparations and to send him my felicitous greetings for the season, but he did not reply, nor were my letters returned. It was as if he had disappeared from the face of the earth.

It was the second time in my life I felt such an enormous loss for someone I loved. I was again alone.

It was on a cold winter's evening when I heard a tapping on the window by the courtyard. Sister Ann was in services, and I was allowed to sit in my room and quietly read. Ann knew my heart was broken, and she let me grieve in my own way.

After climbing over Ann's bed, I pushed the curtain aside. It was dark outside. I moved my candle closer to the window and there to my horror, I saw a man's face through the pane.

It was followed by incessant tapping and waving which made me recoil. Had demons come to find me?

A muffled sound managed through the glass, "Mary, Mary! It's me. Marco. Mary, it's Marco!"

I squinted and leaned closer to the glass. Yes! Yes! It was Marco.

I pulled the window open, confused and amazed in equal measure. Marco climbed through. His face looked blue. I placed a chair by the small wooden stove that was in the corner and instructed him to sit.

"How are you *here*?" I asked in amazement.

But Marco was frozen and shivering. I grabbed my blanket from my bed, put it around his shoulders, and sat on the stone floor waiting for him to thaw. I watched him intently, praying any color beyond blue would return to his face.

Gently, I removed his soaked boots and wet woolen socks. Rubbing his frozen feet, I told him, "You should be better soon," but in my heart, I was not so sure. My mind spun in a thousand directions. Was I dreaming all this?

A long silence passed between us. Finally, he said without any provocation, "I will not marry Christina."

I felt an unusual lightness in my head. I was overjoyed by the news. But cautiously I asked, "Why is that?"

But he ignored my question and simply continued, "They are looking for me now. I do not think they will find me here." He was shivering now. Something had him frightened. I had never known Marco to be frightened.

Looking at me with his beautiful blue eyes, he said, "I came back to you, my Mary," and smiled. Then, reaching down, he grabbed my hand and held it in his.

I can't say how long we stayed that way with me kneeling on the floor and Marco holding my hand as he sat on the chair in front of the cast iron stove. It was the creaking of the door that startled us both and brought us back to the present moment. It was Ann.

We both stood up and turned toward the door. She dropped her books at the sight of us. "Why are you here?" she asked in the most accusatory tone I ever heard her utter.

Marco handed me the blanket that served as his robe. He walked toward Ann, scooped down to gather her books, and handed them back to her. She took them but was unmoved.

"Why are you here?" she repeated.

A heaviness descended into the room, and Marco took a long step back.

"He was frozen outside, and I let him in to warm up by the stove," I said angrily. Surely Ann would be just as pleased and awed as I was.

Quietly and carefully, she walked to her desk, and placed her books down. In a most accusatory tone, which perplexed me, she asked, "Did you ask him to come here?"

"No," he offered in my defense. "No. Mary did not know. No one knows I am here. I had nowhere else to go."

"Shouldn't you be married by now?" she asked, perturbed again.

"He's not going to marry Christina," I said in his defense.

Ann just shook her head and, in a frantic tone, asked, "Where is your coat? Fetch your coat. You cannot stay here."

"I lost it on the freight ship." Marco wrapped his arms around himself.

Ann softened her tone. "Use that blanket for now. Mary, get some kindling. We'll light you a fire in your room in the tower. Mary, bring a candle and a lantern. It will be dark in the stairwell."

Without further discussion, we started off for the bell tower in the cold, starless night. I had not been there during the night before. It held an eerie air. It was not as welcoming as it had been in the spring or summer. Now it seemed a closed-off thing, annoyed we had the poor sense to disturb it.

We climbed the spiral stairs. A cold bitter wind bellowed through the tower, and a bright full moon escaped from the cloud and helped us find our footing to Marco's door. The door moaned open. Sister Ann entered first and placed her candle on the dresser. She quickly lit the oil lamps, and a gentle glow filled the room. I made Marco's bed as I always did. I placed the kindling in the fireplace and watched the first log burn.

"I trust you can take it from here," Ann addressed Marco, and then, sternly, "We will discuss this in the morning. I see no need to wake Mother Superior at this hour." Then, turning to me, she said, "Come, Mary."

On the walk back to our quarters, Ann scowled. "Did you know he was coming, Mary? Tell me if you knew!"

"No. Of course I didn't know!" I yelled as vicious wind grabbed my throat and I raised my collar to keep the draft from reaching down my spine.

"This is not a good thing, Mary. This is a very bad thing. Marco should not be here. This is an ill omen."

I turned and looked behind me at the window that was Marco's room in the tower as it emanated a yellow glow. *Marco found his way back to me* was the only thought that entered my mind. I quickened my pace to catch up with Ann as an owl shrieked in the distance.

Ann and I walked without speaking the rest of the way to our rooms. I was not used to Ann's displeasure with me, and although it disturbed me, I did not want to know of Marco's adventures. He said he had come back. He said he had come back to me!

Oh, when would the sun rise so I could return to him. I did not care about the particulars. I did not care about Christina. He was mine now. Finally and completely mine. That was all that mattered.

45

Chapter 7

I awoke to mumbling sounds outside my door. By the tones, I could tell there was an argument. We never argued in the convent. Ours was a peaceful and jovial existence.

I got out of bed and, pressing my ear against the door, I could hear Sister Ann and Mother Superior in a heated debate.

"He cannot stay here." It was Ann. "You know quite well, if he is here now, there is something wrong." Mother Superior did not reply. Ann continued, "This is wrong. I told you when the boy came here years ago! This falls on our heads. But you would not listen, Margaret. No. No, you would not hear me."

"The bishop asked me to hide him. Where else better than as a convent gardener?"

"He is twisting Mary's heart. Do you think she knows who he is?" Ann asked. "Mary is a young woman, Margaret. And he is a young man. A young, desperate man, who has gotten himself in a lot of trouble . . . "

"Ann, I think you might be over complicating things," was Mother Superior's response "No one knows he's here."

"You're putting us all at considerable risk. And more importantly, Mary! I think she's falling for him. It's gone beyond friendship, Margaret. There's a look in her eyes you would not understand. It's how I looked at Matthew . . .'"

It was at this moment I opened the door. Ann's assumptions of my feelings were too embarrassing for me to allow her to continue exposing them.

"Mary," Mother Superior addressed me surprised. Then looking at Ann and clearing her throat she asked, "Did you know that Marco was coming here?"

"No," I answered.

"Isn't he to be married?" she asked sternly.

"He said he will not marry the girl, Christina," I said.

"When did you become aware of this, child? Did he tell you in a letter?" she asked.

"No. I received no letter from Marco. Not since he left in the summer. I am relieved to know he's well," I said indignantly, which caused Ann to stare at me in annoyance.

"Did he ask for money, Mary?" Ann asked pointedly.

"Why would he ask *me* for money? I have no money. I have no family. This is why I live here," I said, irritated by it all.

"Well, then, I suppose we should talk to Marco," Mother Superior concluded.

I grabbed my coat and scurried along after them to the bell tower. Mother Superior did not knock but opened the door with full force and shut it behind Ann and me. We sat outside on the stone bench. We could not hear what was being said as a sudden wind picked up, and the howling made it difficult.

Ann and I shivered in our coats in silence. Looking about, I remarked how the bell tower seemed less formidable during the day.

After some time, Mother Superior opened the door and announced in a loud, clear voice, "I will be informing the bishop of his nephew's whereabouts." Ann followed her down the stairwell, calling a million questions after Mother Superior, mostly insisting that Marco could not stay.

I creaked the door open to find Marco sitting on his bed with the same brown knit sweater from the night before. The embers in the fireplace had gone low. He smiled as soon as he saw me and motioned for me to sit next to him on the bed. I obeyed and placed my hands in my lap. A nervousness overcame me. He took my hand and held it.

"You said last night that you are not marrying Christina," I said.

He nodded.

"Why?" I asked.

A serious look came upon his face, and, tilting his head, he asked, "Mary, do you remember the day by the beach when I thought you might die?"

I never really thought of that day as one when I had come close to death, but rather one when Marco almost had. I replayed the moment on the beach in my mind so many times in the months that followed.

"Remember that I kissed you?" he asked intently.

How could I possibly forget? It was the first kiss I ever received. It was the first time, I felt what it meant to be loved by a man. I hesitantly nodded.

"It was during confession in preparation for marriage, Christina heard me tell the priest. She got very angry. And she said I was unfaithful to her. She wanted to know if I wanted to marry her. I thought about it at that very moment. And, I knew in my heart, the answer was no."

"You told her no?" I asked, my eyes wide.

"Her brothers did not like this very much. They said I have disgraced the family and vowed my death. I have also disgraced my family, all for you Mary. Because I want to be with you not Christina." He turned my hands in his and stroked them gently. "I came here. No one will find me here."

I looked down at my feet. I did not know how to respond. I did not want to be the cause of Marco's shame and exile.

"The truth is Mary," and here he waited to determine his next words with caution, "as beautiful as Christina is and as wealthy, I hold another in my heart. I have held this other woman in my heart since she fell and broke her ankle, and she became my *bella giovane signora*. I just don't know if she feels the same way."

He leaned over then and kissed me. My second kiss in my entire life. His lips were as soft as I remembered. Slowly, he removed my coat from my shoulders. He rubbed my arms. His touch was so gentle. He kissed my neck. Soft gentle kisses. I could felt my entire body tingle.

He whispered into my ear now, "Mary, tell me that you love me."

I had never told any man I loved them. No man had ever told me that he loved me. Taking a stuttered breath, I managed to whisper back, "I love you, Marco."

My mind began to swirl to a million places. My heart began to beat faster than I'd ever felt it beat before. I closed my eyes and felt his gentle kisses down my neck, and then came the knock at the door.

Startled, Marco stood up and walked to the door, while I caught my breath dazed. When he opened the door, we saw Ann again.

"Mother Superior would like to see you now," she said angrily to Marco. Tossing him an old woolen coat she instructed, "Put this on. It's cold outside. We can't have you catching your death."

She saw I was on the bed. "Mary," she said concerned, "you look quite flushed. Are you getting ill? Is it the shock of it all?" more gently now, she instructed, "Grab your coat and best you come back with me. We'll leave Marco and Mother Superior to sort this all out."

I stood up and gathered my coat from the floor where it had fallen and walked past Marco. My heart was still beating quickly, and I was still short of breath. Ann let me leave the room first and start down the stairs. She then waited for Marco. I could hear his footsteps behind me and the echo of her closing his door. I felt an uneasiness, like Judas, the betrayer.

When we returned to our room after depositing Marco at Mother Superior's office, Ann closed the door and stood squarely in front of me. "You should stay away from Marco," she said matter-of-factly. "He is not who you think he is."

"That is ludicrous! He's the bishop's nephew!" I exclaimed, shaking my head. "I have known Marco since I was a young girl. Why would I stay away from him now?"

"I'm not sure what it is, Mary," she said, "but something is not right. He would go to the bishop before he hopped a ship to come here. I think he has put us and this entire convent in a precarious situation. He's come here without the bishop's blessings for certain; otherwise, Mother Superior would have known. He has gotten too comfortable here, I think." Now Ann began to pace with her habit bobbing up and down in her anger. "He has family. There is absolutely no reason for him to come here."

"Of course, there's reason!" I shouted. "He has me! I am like his family. Why wouldn't he come here?"

Ann stared at me and in a low voice said, "Something's changed Mary," she said plainly. "And neither you nor I know what it is."

"I know what it is." I stomped my foot like a small child. "Marco loves me. He told me. He loves me, and he came for me."

"He loves you? Came for you? Came for you to do what?" Ann asked incredulously.

"I don't know," I said exasperated. Why was Ann being so difficult? Why could she not be happy for me? Why could she not sit on the edge of her bed, as she did when I was child, and listen?

Oh, how I wished she was not angry with me. How I wished I could have told her that Marco kissed me. How I wished I could have told her, that I felt peculiar now when he was near me, that my mind had twisted itself, and my heart would not stop quickening its pace. But no, Ann did not want to hear. She folded her arms and looked out the window by her bed. She was not interested in anything I had to say.

We fell silent. And although we stayed together the rest of the day, we did not address each other. In silence we took our meals in our room, read our books, and prepared to slumber.

I never had experienced Ann's disapproval, and I was ill prepared to receive it. All these years, Ann had always been with me to guide me and teach me and stand with me. But not this time. This time she was distant. She was lost in her own world.

She was right. Something had changed. *I* had changed. I could only think of Marco. I could only think of going back to his room. I could only think of how I felt when he stroked my arms and kissed me. I yearned to feel that again. It was madness that had overtaken me.

That night, I waited until I knew that Ann would be fast asleep. With my coat over my sleeping gown, I lit a small oil lantern to take with me and crept out of the room. I did not care about the sounds that ordinarily would have scared me in the darkness, or the shadows that passed by the full moon. I had one singular thought, and that was Marco. I could think of nothing more than being near him again.

When I finally arrived at the bell tower and ascended the stairs, I felt a strange trepidation. As if, for only a moment my better mind had reappeared. *Go back, Mary,* it warned just like it had that fateful day by the shore, but madness when it fully takes root, cannot easily be tamed.

Finally, I stood before the door. I knocked lightly and waited. Perhaps he was asleep? "Marco!" I whispered. "Marco, it's Mary. I know it's late . . . "

I slowly lifted the latch and opened the door. It was dark, except for the light of my lantern and a gentle glow of embers in the fireplace.

"Marco!" I whispered, "Are you asleep?"

Carefully, I closed the door behind me and started to walk towards his bed. And then I felt it. A cold blade across my throat, as an arm reached back and pulled me towards the window.

"Who are you?!" the voice shouted.

"Mary," I said weakly.

Immediately the blade fell to the ground, and I was spun around to see the shadow of Marco's face as he held me tight. "Mary!" He began to weep. "Mary, I almost . . . I almost . . . "

"Why do you have a knife? Where did you get it?" I was terrorized.

"I always have a knife hidden under the bed. It's been there for years, Mary."

"No," I said pulling away. "I clean this room every year after you leave. There has never been a knife in this room."

"I thought you were someone else," he said simply adding, "I'm sorry, Mary." Moving my hair from the side of my face he whispered. "I'm glad it is you." Leaning in he kissed.

Again, I was intoxicated. Completely defenseless.

After moving me over closer to the window he removed my coat and dropped it on the floor. He inspected me in the moonlight. "You are beautiful, Mary. You are a woman now, and you are beautiful."

I blushed. After lifting me up to carry me as he had done so many times when I was younger, he placed me gently on the bed and said in a whisper, "You will always be my Mary."

Chapter 8

I awoke slightly before dawn, cradled in Marco's arms. I could feel his breath gently fall on my face as I watched his bare chest rise and fall. I tried to rise without waking Marco and gather my things. Slowly I began to dress, trying in my mind to fully comprehend what had transpired the night before.

"You are beautiful in the morning," Marco said, and, when I turned around, I saw him smile. I was still dazed by it all. No one had ever explained this all to me. I had been raised by women. Not once did the conversation about the nature of men and women ever come to a dialogue.

I suppose there was no need. I never ventured out of the safety of the convent. All those who visited the convent never came to see me. Quickly they would receive their remedies, candles, prayers, whatever they needed, and they would promptly depart. I was always in the company of women. I was utterly unprepared. We were all unprepared.

"Come here and sit with me." He tapped the bed and motioned me over. Moving my hair behind my ear and taking my hand again, he asked, "Do you love me? Would you do anything for me?" He looked at me more intently now, desperate for an answer.

I started to tear. "Yes. Of course. Whatever you ask of me."

Marco continued, "Because, now it's different. You understand that right?"

I nodded in affirmation.

"Mary, since I know now you will love me as a woman, I have something I must give you." Wrapping a sheet around his torso, he went back to his carpet bag and pulled out a small satin blue bag like the one he gave me the year before. Opening it and kneeling on one knee, he placed a thin, plain gold band on my finger. "When my uncle comes, he will marry us. We are one now." Rising, he embraced me again.

I remember the uneasiness and awkwardness of it all. I never thought about marriage, or what marriage meant. I was so young. So inexperienced. So lost in a new world for which I was unprepared. As I think of it now, he never asked me. He told me. He told me we were to be married, and I, in my naïveté, did not stop to consider it.

The sun began to brighten the horizon. "I must hurry before Ann knows I've gone." I started to put on my coat.

"I will go with you. We will tell her together." He stood and started to dress.

"No. I'll tell her. I'll tell her soon. Sleep. I must get back, before she notices I'm gone. I will see you at breakfast. Let's not tell anyone yet." After he kissed me one more time, I departed.

I did not tell Ann about my ring as I knew she would not approve, and I so desperately wanted to have her approval. Instead, I removed the band and hid it in my pocket.

But Marco did not make it to breakfast that morning or for any other meal with us. Mother Superior instructed Marco to simply stay in the tower and out of sight until she had heard back from his uncle, the bishop. For the next few evenings, when Ann fell asleep, I would quietly leave and go to be with Marco, remembering to place the ring on my finger when I arrived. It was on one such evening that Marco asked me about my past and my fortune.

My head resting on his shoulder, he asked, "Mary, why did you not tell you were a Whitcombe?"

That was a name I never used. I never referred to myself as anything other than Mary. Whitcombe was a foreign sound to me. I never used it. It brought forth the shrill sounds of my nanny calling it up the stairs with venom in her breath. Whitcombe on her lips became an insult and a curse.

"What?" I asked.

"How much of your fortune is left?" he asked coldly.

I laughed. "I don't know what you mean about a fortune." I lifted my head and stretched my neck to kiss him. But he moved away.

"The money your father left," he said seriously.

"I don't even remember my father," I laughed again balancing my head on my bent arm.

"We will need money to live," he said. "After we are married, we will need to live somewhere. We cannot stay in the bell tower forever."

I hadn't thought of such practical measures. I was still caught in the love affair of Marco wanting to be with me. He was the only man I'd known since I was young girl. And he had grown to have affections for me, as I did him. There was nothing more I needed than to go there each evening and fall asleep in Marco's arms. Whatever he desired of me, I would give.

"I don't know, Marco. I never asked," I said plainly. "Everything I've ever wanted, I found here. This has been my home since I was a little girl. I never thought about leaving it or needing to leave it. I don't know anything about a fortune or being a Whitcombe."

"But you are a Whitcombe," he insisted.

"Yes."

"The only living heir to Whitcombe fortune, yes?"

"Yes." I shrugged my shoulders.

"All these years you said nothing." He continued, "I did not need Christina if I had you."

"You needed her for what?" I asked anxiously.

Now Marco sat up and started to scold me, "Mary. Why are you being this way? What did you think would happen when you became a woman? You would get married and live here among the nuns with your children and husband?"

"I never thought about getting married." I rested on my elbow as I looked up at his beautiful face. "Or children."

"Someone must know about your money. Mother Superior is hiding it."

"Mother Superior? Now why would she do that?" To change the mood, I said coyly, "Marco, you need to kiss me again. I fear I'm getting cold." He held his distance.

"You're frightening me. Why are you so angry?"

"I'm sorry, Mary. Forgive me. I am not myself. I have many thoughts in my mind. Thoughts about my future. Your future. Come sit by the fire." No other word passed between us that evening. There was a frigidness that no fire could warm. A cold calcification descended on my heart.

It was early the next morning when a banging on the door awoke Marco and me.

"Marco!" It was Sister Ann's voice, and a panic overtook me. "Have you seen Mary?" The banging continued.

I did not wake up early enough to make it back to my room! Marco's unsettling behavior weighed heavy on my mind.

Sleep came late and I did not rise by first light. Marco was not disturbed. He wrapped the sheet around his torso again and walked to the door.

"Marco! What are you doing?" I scrambled to find my coat. Opening the door halfway, he smiled broadly. "Sister Ann! Good morning!"

Ann tried to cover her face and look down at the stone tiles, noting that Marco was without proper attire. He had never done that before.

He relished her embarrassment. "Yes, I have seen Mary. She's right there on the bed." He swung the door open fully so Ann could see me.

I will never forget the look that crossed Ann's face. It was one of sadness, horror and disappointment.

"It's alright, Ann!" I tried to reassure her as she saw me there in my undergarments. "We are going to be married. Marco gave me a ring!" And here I showed my hand with the gold band that Marco had given me.

Ann stood by the doorway, looking at me, then, looking at Marco, who was grinning. I could see her heart break.

After some time, she addressed me only, "Mary, I want you to get dressed and come with me. I will wait outside the door." She closed it behind her.

I glared at Marco. How humiliating to open that door so quickly without warning. How hurt Ann looked and how triumphant Marco looked. This was not the Marco I knew.

I dressed and found Ann waiting for me outside the door. She didn't speak, but simply turned and started down the stairs to exit the bell tower.

"Aren't you happy for me?" I asked when we reached the bottom of the tower steps. "I'm going to be married. Marco is going to ask the bishop when he comes. We can get married right here in our church, Ann! Won't it be wonderful? I'd like to wait to spring, though, so I can hold the flowers that have been growing in Marco's garden for so long!"

Ann was not moved at all. She just looked solemn. I waited for her to reply, but she said nothing

"Ann, you know how much I care for Marco! All these *years*! You wanted me to go out in the world and have a life of my own, and I will! And I love Marco, like you loved your husband!" But again, Ann said nothing. "Please say something. Ann! Please!"

We marched back in the cold with nothing more said between us. When we arrived in our rooms, a heavy silence fell around us. I looked at Ann's face. She had been crying. Her tear drops had frozen on her face.

Sitting on the edge of her bed with her hands in her lap now, Ann simply said, "I don't know what to say, Mary. I do wish you waited for everything to be sorted. Or I wish you had talked to me, at the very least. I always thought you would." And, looking down at her hands, she said the last words with disappointment.

"Ann, I'm telling you now!" I said, excited again.

"No, Mary. You have done a very foolish thing with Marco. You don't understand." Here she stopped. "I always thought I would have time to talk about these things with you, about men and women and nature, and life outside these walls. We thought we'd have time to take you out and let . . . I didn't think you'd want to take your vows, but . . . We—none of us ever assumed . . . that, Mary, you would have . . ." And she could not say it. She could not say the thing she wanted most to say to me.

But, in truth, I did not care. I had grown from a child into a woman in what seemed like moments. I knew what it was to be wanted by a man. Life would be forever different. I had no remorse. I did not feel a need for penitence or whatever emotions of regret or pity that Ann was expressing.

It was a mere hour when another decree came from Mother Superior that I was forbidden to see Marco. I was not to be left alone under any circumstance. I was to be escorted everywhere by one of the sisters. Even Sister Maxine was assigned to keep watch by the door. I was a prisoner. But I did not care, for I knew the bishop would come, and he would marry us. Marco and I would be together for an eternity.

It was on the seventh day of my confinement that Mother Superior came to see me and Ann.

"Mary," she began in her stern way, "Marco has come to see me about your inheritance." She began to pace the room, formulating her next words. "What have you told him about your fortune, child?"

I shrugged my shoulders. "I don't know anything about my fortune."

She nodded, pacing again and taking a deep breath. "How did he know about it? Did you tell him you were the heir to the Whitcombe fortune?"

"No," I answered. In truth, I had never heard anything about a Whitcombe fortune.

"It is curious to me," Mother Superior continued, "how he's come to know of it."

After a long pause, I asked, "Do I have a fortune? Am I an heir of some sort? Were the Whitcombes wealthy?"

A strange look came over Mother Superior. A look I had never seen before and could not place. Her eyes became smaller, and her mouth tightened, and she stared at me as if newly vexed. She did not answer me and simply walked out the door.

I asked Ann, "Do I have a fortune?"

"I don't know, Mary." She sounded perplexed. Raising her eyebrows slightly, she concluded, "I never thought of it. I just cared for you."

"But if I have a fortune, why was I left here?"

"I don't know, Mary. I didn't ask many questions when Mother Superior told me you were coming. I was just happy to have you with me."

"I don't understand any of it," I said.

Ann resumed folding her linens, "You are a grown woman now, Mary. It struck me hard at first, as you will always be a child in my eyes. But I cannot keep you here. The bishop will be here the night after tomorrow. Marco has insisted that he will marry you no matter what Mother Superior has said to him."

Here, for the first time in many days, her face softened. "You're both persistent in that way. Foolish and persistent, but I suppose that's the blessing of youth." Then, after a breath, she continued, "It seems foolish to keep you cloistered away now. Go tell Marco you will be married tomorrow. I hope you both find joy in this lifetime."

I embraced Ann tightly, and she said, "I will always love you, Mary, like you were my own. Remember to come see me with your children when you settle into your life." She smiled for the first time in days. I felt the overwhelming boulder of disapproval lift from my shoulders. All had been forgiven.

We held each other then, both hopeful for life that was to come.

It was midday when I left to find Marco. The sun shone brightly in the sky, and there was a light powder of fresh white snow covering the ground in a gentle blanket. I remember how wonderful the cold air felt as it filled my lungs. There was excitement and a newness to it all. My life was about to begin. I was to be Marco's wife. By tomorrow's sunrise, I would leave the convent, and Marco and I would be together as man and wife. These thoughts filled my mind as I pranced along, picking up bits of snow and throwing them in the air.

As I came closer to the tower, I noted several sets of larger footprints in the snow that led to the tower gate. They were not markings of any shoes that the sisters wore. Looking up, I was perplexed as to why Marco would have left his window open in the cold. Any quick gust would extinguish the flame.

I did not know why, but a deep pain began to form in my stomach. I felt a strange sense of apprehension. "Marco!" I yelled as I came to the stairwell. The sound of my voice reverberated back to me with no response.

I started to climb the twisted gray stone staircase. My heart beat faster with each step. "Marco!" I called again. No reply.

Halfway there, I stopped. There was a newspaper clipping on the floor. It was brown with age. I bent down to pick it up. The headline read, "William and Grace Whitcombe Lost at Sea." And there was a picture. My parents!

I held the delicate parchment close to my heart in an embrace. A tear escaped and landed on the stone step.

"Marco?" I called again, unsure of myself as I climbed the stairs more slowly now. Were these little surprises left for me from Marco? Were they my wedding gift?

A few more steps. There on the stone was a faded lithograph of a small baby in the arms of a woman. I flipped it over and read on the back, written in a small hand, "Grace and Mary. April." A chill ran down my spine, and I started to tear. Where did he find them? Where did he find these relics from a life I barely remembered?

I climbed the top of the staircase, and right outside Marco's door was my last offering. It was a torn letter with only two words visible "Whitcombe fortune."

Looking up, I saw Marco's door was wide open. "Marco," I said with joy. "Marco, I found these things outside."

Holding the pieces of my past in my hands, I continued, "Do you know how they came to appear? Are these gifts to me?"

Marco was lying in his bed, with this back towards the door as I entered.

"Marco? Marco, are you sleeping?" I smiled, placing my finds on the small table by the open window and closed it to warm the room, I continued, "I don't know where you found these treasures, but they mean the world to me. Sister Ann finally released me from my confinement."

I turned around to him again. "Come, Marco I think you've carried this on a bit too far now."

I walked over to the bed now. Trying to roll him over gently, I saw it. I saw the red stream of blood that poured from his chest and soaked the bed. Standing up, I screamed in horror.

His eyes, his beautiful blue eyes, lifeless, stared at me. Bending down again toward him, not understanding what I was seeing, I whispered again, "Marco?" The tears began to fall from my face. "Marco?" I said louder, and now with my hands covered in his blood, I could not bear it all and screamed even louder, "Marco!" collapsing to the floor.

It was a firm hand that grasped by shoulders. "Stand up, child!" the voice ordered. Someone raised me to my legs, placing arms around me, and I was led out the door of Marco's room. The wind blew across my face from the bell tower, and I found my breath belabored.

"I can't," I said, falling to my knees. "I can't breathe." I collapsed on the floor, the cold stone as my last memory.

Chapter 9

I remember awaking to Ann's face hovering over me.

"God blessed!" She said, "Mary's eyes are opening!"

I was back in my room, with Sister Ann in a chair next to me with her arm on my forehead and Sister Maxine and Sister Francine standing around her. It was Sister Francine who spoke next, "You hit your head hard, child."

When? I thought. *How did I end up here? Where was I before?* My eyes darting around the room, I remembered. I was with Marco. Sitting up, suddenly in a panic with tears forming in my eyes, I felt my breath catch. Was that an awful dream?

"Marco?" I whispered.

It was sister Maxine who spoke now. "He's dead, child. A stab wound to the chest. They have called the constable, who will want to speak to you."

"Mother Superior found you," Sister Francine offered. "You fainted."

"I was looking for you," Ann continued apologetically, "but Mother Superior found you first. She said she heard you scream and came to find you. Did anyone hurt you?" Her voice was one of concern, and tears began to form. Cradling my head in her arms, she began to weep.

"Drink this child," Sister Maxine said, handing me a warm cup of what seemed to be an odd-smelling tea. Staring up into her eyes, I saw a sadness I had never seen before. Obeying, I took a sip and remarked, "It's bitter."

"Drink it all, Mary," Sister Francine instructed with an equally sad look.

Through the door, I heard Mother Superior's muffled voice first "There were artifacts everywhere about Mary's fortune."

And a man's voice in return said, "It won't matter now."

"How could he have possibly known?" Mother Superior asked in a panic. "It puts us all at risk now, doesn't it? My entire convent at risk because of *that* boy and *that* girl."

But there was no answer in return. Instead, the door opened, and the bishop walked into the room. All the sisters genuflected, and I just sat on the edge of my bed.

After taking off his collar and placing his miter on the bed beside me, he sat down next to me, his eyes near to tears, and, turning to the sisters in the room, he simply ordered, "Leave us."

Slowly standing, they stared at the bishop in partial disbelief, to which he repeated, "Leave us." Like scolded school children, they slowly made it to the door and, after looking back at the bishop to determine his resolve, left the room. It was Mother Superior who stood indignant by the door the longest, with her hands clasped together in front of her.

"You too, Margaret," he said.

A look of anger crossed her face, but before she could reply, he raised his hand to silence her. And here a stalemate ensued. Mother Superior with her steely gaze and the bishop returning in kind, his blue eyes the same color as Marco's, and his willfulness intact. He did not waver. Finally, Mother

Superior broke her resolve. When she exited the door, she slammed it shut.

"Mary," the bishop began. "My nephew was a troubled boy. I had hoped that by spending time with the good sisters here, he would find his way." He tried to find the words to follow.

"He often spoke of you, Mary. You inspired him to seek better things in life. And I know in my heart he loved you deeply." Here, touching his hand to his temple, he lowered his head to shield his eyes. But I saw the teardrop betray him and stain his garment.

He continued, "I'm very sorry if he ever took advantage of your better nature, Mary. I know you were an innocent." Here his voice faltered. "Any sin that befell you is mine now. I absolve you of it."

Standing up and gathering his things, he turned and said this, "You can stay here as long as you desire. I care not what Margaret says. If you should ever find yourself in any need, or if you find yourself ever ill-treated here, or anywhere in your life's journey, you simply need to write, and I will grant you whatever assistance I am able to provide. I solemnly swear that on my life." He stood now and muttered a prayer over me and signed the cross.

Twisting the fabric of my skirt in my finger, I only uttered, "We were to be married." These were the last words I would speak for two years.

Chapter 10

I did not know that Sister Ann was ill. Aside from a persistent cough, I did not concern myself. I was too lost in my own grief and anger in the last two years to think of anything other than my sorrow.

The bishop never returned. The bell tower ceased to ring, and the room where Marco had lived for so many summers was sealed. Only the flowers by the fountain in the courtyard persisted, as I would water and prune the roses, remembering whatever Marco had taught me.

My studies ceased. And life at the convent resumed without me. I was a ghost that passed in the shadows of the dormitories and rooms and hallways. I did not go to services or prayers any longer. I did not read the scriptures. I ceased to wear the uniforms of the convent and instead chose my own simple dresses ordered in a catalog and paid for by the convent.

Mine was a solitary and silent life. I would take my easel and paints and find myself absorbed in whatever subject I studied. I would wander through the woods and take quiet trips down to the ocean. Everywhere I looked, there was the ghost of Marco. The place on the sand where we had our first lunch. The place where he kissed me. It was all there. Every memory. Every moment. Every word we uttered between us was trapped among the corridors I wandered, lingering on the wing of every butterfly that flew by me, present in every petal that fell from the roses. It was there, all around me.

I found no comfort. No solace. No reprieve. It was an omnipotent sadness that locked my heart into that moment, that moment when I felt the loss so deep in my soul, I found no reason to climb out ever again.

It was when the third winter came since Marco's murder that I noticed Sister Ann seemed thinner and frailer. She labored more when she walked and sat resting in a chair more often. She began to diminish. Her cough persisted in the evenings, often causing me to wake. She stopped waking up for morning prayers.

It was early December when she broke into a fever that never ceased, and with each breath came a strange sound as if the air in her lungs were desperately trying to escape through the narrowest of passages. I sat by her bed and changed the wet cloths on her forehead in an attempt to alleviate the fevers. I placed pillows behind her head to elevate her torso in an effort to help her breathe.

No remedy that Sister Maxine would bring seemed to cure, however foul-tasting or smelling. Even the doctor with his pills and potions found nothing to aid her, and, in a solemn act of placing his stethoscope in his bag, he simply offered, "Keep her as comfortable as you can, Mary." There was nothing more he could do.

It seems that grief compounds upon grief, and the thought of Sister Ann, the only mother I knew, passing away, compelled me to speak. Holding her hand, I said quietly, "I am very sorry I disappointed you with my actions with Marco. I did not know . . . "

"Shhh," she managed to say between belabored breaths, "the fault . . . the fault is mine." And another labored breath. "I did not warn you about men. I never thought . . . " But here a coughing fit overtook her and shook her body violently. Blood began to issue from her mouth. Horrified, I opened the door and called for anyone to come.

She died that night. We were alone. I sat there with her and held her hand. Wiping the blood that would trickle from her mouth. Giving her sips of broth or tea or whatever she desired.

I told her I loved her, that I loved her like no other. I reminded her of the games we played when I was a little girl. I thanked her for taking me in. I thanked her for loving me as no other person could. I thanked her for all the things she was to me. I thanked her for teaching me to draw and for my art.

I asked her to stay with me a little longer, and she tried. She tried with all her might, but as the sun rose, she took her very last breath. And I sobbed.

I sobbed in a way I had never done before. There, lying on her corpse, I cried from the very depth of my soul. I cried for the loss of my mother, my father, my sister, Marco and Ann. There was so much loss in such a little lifetime time. I was only twenty years, but I felt like there was nothing left for me in life.

I cried until her garments were soaked with my tears, and I could not produce any more, and I could not utter another sound of despair. There was nothing left for me now. There was nothing left for me at the convent or anywhere in life.

It was late morning when the bedroom door opened and Sister Francine entered with a tray for breakfast but seeing Ann's corpse and my head placed across her chest as I slumped in my chair, she dropped the tray in horror. Raising her hands to cover her mouth, she began to sob. She pulled me from Ann and, sitting me upright in the chair, and being small of stature she held my head to her chest. Stroking my hair, she whispered, "She's with God now, child. She is with God."

She held me there for some time before she reached into the pocket of her black gown and gave me a letter. Ann wrote this for you many months ago when she thought she might not recover. She asked me to keep this for you and give it to you when she passed."

After handing me the letter, she walked over to the scattered toast, tea, broken plate and teacup, and honey, and placed it back on the tray. Standing, she said, "I'll inform the others, but I will give you time to read the letter," and quietly she exited the door.

I fumbled with the letter in my shaking hand.

My Dearest Mary,

From the moment you came into my life, I knew you were a blessing. I want you to know that I have felt so very lucky to care for you all these years. I have watched you grow into the beautiful woman you are now.

I know you have suffered many losses that have been incredibly unfair. It is more than any one person should have to bear. But know that I have always been steadfast in my love for you. Any disappointing tone or scolding you may have received from me was because of my own failings.

In my heart, I know there is a someone out there in the greater world who will love you for you and not your fortune. Raise your head high, Mary. You are not only my daughter, but you are indeed a Whitcombe.

In some way, I hope you may come to understand the philanthropic family into which you were born. This convent and church are a testament to their generous nature. In many ways, Mary, this place and all the lands belong to you, and we are all merely guests.

I have made arrangements that, a week from my passing, there will be an art show for you to sell your paintings—all those paintings from all those years we kept in storage. Once I die, your name as the artist will be displayed in all the papers so that many will come.

I want you to collect the profits and chart your life. Too long, I've kept you here in these walls. Go find your life, Mary. You have been a great daughter, but there is nothing left for you here now.

Know there is always hope, and if you ever find yourself in doubt, pray, and God will answer you.

Affectionately,
Your second mother, Ann.

It was late afternoon when Sister Ann's body was boarded on a wagon and plans made for her funeral. She left instructions to be buried with her beloved Matthew. As I watched the casket jostle in the carriage and disappear down on the road. Mother Superior summoned me into her office. In all my time, at the convent, I had only been there a few times before for minor infractions and punishments, which Ann always argued away. It was Ann who raised me and kept Mother Superior at a distance.

I knocked and heard permission to enter. I opened the heavy creaking door into the small square-shaped room made of the same grey jagged stone of the dormitories. Before me stood Mother Superior behind a large dark wooden desk, her arms underneath her habit, a large silver crucifix behind her. Her countenance imposing.

"Sit, Mary." She gestured to a chair in front of me, a stern, unsympathetic look in her eyes.

Shaking my head, I simply said, "I'd rather not."

More gently now, she said, "We are all saddened by the passing of Sister Ann. She loved you very much. But a time has come now where you need to make a choice."

"A choice?" I asked, half dismayed.

"Yes. A choice. We let you live here, while Ann was alive, but it is time for you to decide if you'd like to join our order or not."

"Let me live here? I had no choice but to live here."

"This was not a prison, Mary. You have always been free to go."

"Free to go where? To the woods? To the water? Where was I free to go?"

"You will need to choose, Mary."

"Choose to join your order?" I asked in disbelief. "Are you telling me I need to be a nun, or I need to leave?"

She stared at me.

"This has been my home since I was a girl."

"You are not a girl now," was her only response.

"Ann said that these walls were more mine than yours."

Here, her face grew pale for a moment, and a flash of anger crossed her face.

"Ann is not here," was her only reply, followed by, "I'll need an answer."

I was angry now. "You do know the bishop said, if you were ever to ask anything of me that I did not like, I was to reach out straight away."

"You insolent, child!" she exclaimed, banging her fist on the table.

"I thought you said I was not a child." I replied.

Gaining her composure she asked again, "Do you want to join this order?"

"No," I said in defiance. "No. I do not. I will leave but on my terms." She sat down in her chair, anxiously awaiting my next reply.

"I will leave in two weeks' time, after the art show that Ann arranged." A look of confusion crossed her face. "I don't think she told you, but it's been arranged. I will take my earnings and leave." As I started to walk out the door, I stopped and closed it again. Turning to Mother Superior, I said, belligerently, "I want what is left of my fortune."

Looming over her, I placed my pointed finger on her desk and repeated, "I will leave in two weeks' time, but you need to give me what is left of my fortune."

Defiantly, Mother Superior answered, "I'm not sure what Ann told you before she died, but there is only 200 pounds left, and you are more than welcome to it." Nodding, I turned to leave when she called after me, "It was greed for your fortune that killed Marco."

Leaving the room, I closed the door vowing in my mind to never see Mother Superior again.

Chapter 11

It was a frigid and jouncy carriage ride to the Longs' mansion.
I did not know why then, but it seemed that Judge Long's
interest in my welfare went beyond his wife's love of art, or his
desire to be a patron of the arts. It was rooted much deeper.

It was an odd twist of fate that the Longs came to the
art show. It was odd to me that so many people came. Ann
made sure the advertisements prominently placed the name
"Whitcombe" which I think is what drew the crowd. It was as
if a collective memory was unlocked, and massive mourning
had ensued.

I sold all my paintings. Hundreds of canvases piled up
in the attic of the dormitories had waited for this moment.
Each patron hoped for a small token of something touched
by a Whitcombe. I didn't understand it then, but it meant
something to each of them, for my parents had been exceed-
ingly philanthropic. My paintings served as a reminder of a
more generous time.

It was the judge who approached me first. "You *are* Mary
Whitcombe," he said, stating a fact. "You are indeed." And

a look of recognition came over his face as he continued, "I wanted to know if I might impose on you. I appreciate that this will seem unorthodox, but my wife, Lady Isabella, is a considerable patron of the arts as well as an ardent lover of paintings. She is particularly interested in having her portrait done, and it would oblige me greatly, having studied your work and purchased your renderings, if you would consider painting one of her."

I remember feeling overwhelmed. "Thank you, sir. You flatter me greatly, but I have no studio or place where I paint . . . currently. I'm leaving the convent this evening and will be traveling. My belongings are already packed."

"Pity," Judge Long said. "Is there a way that you might consider delaying your travels for a short period? We would gladly grant you space in our estate. You could have your pick of rooms and light." Then, he gestured to a woman to join us, and, upon her arrival, he offered, "This is Lady Isabella, and I am Judge Frederick Long."

"Oh, *you* are the artist," she said, gushing. Then she turned to Frederick. "I must have her paint me. You must paint me," she said matter-of-factly.

"Well, dear, I have asked, but Miss Whitcombe here has informed me that she will be traveling shortly and cannot accommodate our request."

Although I had not fully considered where I would travel, there was an inn nearby I heard mentioned and my intention was to settle there to begin. I would then send letters inquiring about employment as a governess or instructor being well-versed in many subjects and if all else failed, I'd return to the convent or write the bishop. These were my plans; however roughly sketched in my mind.

It was then that I noticed a small tug at my arm, which belonged to Sister Maxine. She smiled broadly and then nodded at the Longs. It was as if a veil of understanding passed between them.

"Excuse me, Lady and Judge Long, this is Sister Maxine." I introduction them.

"We will pay you handsomely for your work. We will give you the appropriate space. I will not hear of any objections." Lady Isabella said emphatically.

"The Longs," I explained to Sister Maxine, "have offered me employ in their estate as a painter."

Sister Maxine smiled, "You know, Mary. I do believe Sister Ann hoped the Longs might come find you." She hurriedly added, "To see your work." Then slowly, "They are great patrons of the arts as were your parents."

Lady Isabella snapped her fingers, and several gentlemen appeared seemingly out of the ether. And, addressing them, she said, "Fetch whatever articles Miss Whitcombe has onto our carriage and send ahead a message to have the north bedroom readied for her arrival. She will be our guest for the evening."

Then, turning to me and Sister Maxine, she smiled broadly, "There. It's settled." Giving Frederick a look of victory, she turned sharply and allowed the large ostrich feather in her hat to brush his face slightly.

And so, here I was, regarding them both, the guardians it seemed for which Sister Ann hoped. Judge Long was seated to my right, with his distinguished moustache and top hat, his face showing small lines of age. There was a strange longing in his eyes as he stared out of the carriage. His eyes would close ever so slightly as if slumber were his most welcomed companion.

Lady Isabella, who sat across from me, for her part had a stern face with a long, sharp nose that came to a point. Her eyes, although a beautiful shade of blue, seemed uncommon in a face that showed no other signs of beauty. Having recently removed her gloves, she crossed plump hands over her lap. She moved her head like a nervous bird, darting from her searching glances outside the carriage window to Judge Long's face as if she anticipated him speaking at any moment. Her garments clung too closely to her skin, with her bosoms protruding through the top fringe of her blouse.

It was after a while, and what I could only take for Lady Isabella's discomfort, that she spoke to me, startling Judge Long from whatever trance he had adequately transfixed himself in. Clearing her throat, she began, "Mary! I think it is quite wise of you to decide to take on our little arrangement. You will be quite happy with us. And I am sure we will be quite happy with you. Isn't that right, Frederick?"

But not waiting for his reply at all, she continued after taking a deep breath, "You know, I was never able to have children. It has been me and Frederick for all these years in the manor. Only the two of us." She stopped and stared out the window to remember what it was that she wanted to say next. "I did try to have a pet once. A dog. Dreadful thing. It made me painfully ill. I am not suited for any form of animals in the house."

"Remember, darling," Frederick offered, "I did once suggest a bird. A paraquet or perhaps a lovely yellow canary . . . "

Lady Isabella responded with an icy stare. "Quite right. Yes. A bird would not have been the best companion. Therefore, Mary," Lady Isabella continued, "once you settle in this evening, we will begin in helping you better understand refinement." She cocked her head to the side like a paraquet which required me to suppress a smile. "I think we'll need to get you a few new frocks. I'll send word to my person. Yes. In the morning . . . "

But before she could finish her sentence, Judge Long declared that we were arriving at the manor. I leaned over to peer though the small carriage window as the sun began to set. There was an odd figure, a footman, dressed in a strange ornamental costume. I later came to learn it was Lady Isabella's requirement; having come through some royal bloodline at some point, she insisted on things she considered to squarely fall into the category of "refinement."

The manor itself was a gray limestone on a small hill that stretched into the sky. It was stark without ivy growing on the façade, or ornamental flowers in marble vases or trees to surround the property. It was a cold, barren thing that seemed oddly placed in the landscape, as nothing within a several hundred yards would grow near it. It showed no warmth or light. It stood solitary behind a heavy black iron gate. I thought how strange and devoid of life, compared to St. Agnes.

As soon as the carriage entered and we stopped by the entranceway, a footman opened the door. Judge Long departed first, and, offering me his hand, he helped me down the steps. Nodding as he searched my face, he simply whispered "yes" and then turned to help Lady Isabella disembark.

Before me stood an old chestnut wooden door painted the brightest emerald green. I wondered at that moment what twist of fate had me standing here in this strange courtyard with the moon starting to rise above me.

Seeing my concern, Judge Long addressed me, "Yes. The Lady had the door painted. It was part of one of her art projects. She commissioned it, said it was part of elevating the aesthetic." Smiling warmly, he reassured me, "You will be comfortable here, Mary. I will make sure of it."

In contrast to the starkness of the outside of the manor, the inside was a strange amalgamation of oriental vases and oddly placed furnishings, with Persian rugs and strange ornate silk flowers. It was nothing like one would have expected to see in an English manor house. The colors and patterns accosted the senses. The ceiling rose high above to a point with stained-glass windows where the roof should have been. Overlooking the space was a balcony attached to a staircase that came angularly down to where we stood.

"Mary, come here!" It was Lady Isabella who spoke with considerable excitement, moving to the far end of the hall and pulling aside sliding doors that were painted in black lacquer with small white orchids. "This is where I will hang them all."

Frederick nodded at me, informing me it was fine to follow.

Here I saw the nature of Lady Isabella's preoccupation: what should have served as a great dining hall was bare.

"I emptied this room, Mary, so that all your portraits of me could hang here. It would be called 'An Ode to a Lady.' I will start by hanging some of the paintings we purchased this evening. Think of this as your own little museum wing, Mary. This is your gallery now." And, delighted, she darted her head about the room and then rested her eyes on me. "We will have such parties to celebrate your work."

"I hope I don't disappoint you, Lady Isabella. This all seems quite an undertaking I can't imagine the time required to fill such a space," I replied.

Undaunted, she simply answered, "It will be of no concern to me, Mary. I have no expectation of time. I understand the temperament of an artist. Before I met Frederick, I used to be quite close to a number of artists in Paris . . . "

It was Frederick who interrupted, saying gently, "I'm sure Mary is overwhelmed and tired. Perhaps we should show her to her quarters for the evening and have something to eat sent up?"

"I would be ever so grateful," I answered.

Immediately, servant girls appeared to escort me to my quarters. It was an odd procession of people, some carrying my belongings behind me while others held bronze oil lanterns to light the way through creaking floorboards. My room was in the far hall. It was a quiet part of the house, with a wide window that looked out to the vast grasslands with small spots of lavender fields.

It seemed that Lady Isabella's decorative enthusiasm had not come to my room, as it was appointed with tasteful cherry wood furnishings with small ornate carvings, a large post bed and soft ivory linens. There were two wooden night tables adorned with the most beautiful glass oil lamps, each panel decorated with glass lavender tiles forming fireflies, hand-cut and stained. I came to learn later they were important, from America and styled by Louis Comfort Tiffany.

To my left was the most ornate dressing vanity. It contained the largest rounded mirror I had ever seen, and on the counter were powders, hair combs, ribbons, a hand mirror cast in silver and a comb and brush in the same style. There was the softest satin chair that I could not help but touch. To my right were two large dressing cabinets. All I owned in the world could fill half of one drawer. And yet, with all its splendor, I felt oddly at ease, as if I had come home, at least for the moment.

A gentle tapping preceded the opening of my bedroom door, with a young woman about my age entering, balancing a silver tray of food she promptly planted on my vanity. "Sorry, miss, but this was getting heavy. I have on there a nice bowl of soup and some ham, bread and cheese. There's also a warm cup of tea in the pot. I placed a bit of honey there," she concluded pointing to the teapot.

"Yes, thank you," I said.

"Mr. Frederick wouldn't let the Lady decorate your room for your arrival. He had these things placed here thinking they would bring you comfort," she continued. "He did it himself, he did. Saw an ad with your art display and he was a man possessed. It was nice to see a fire in him again. Do you like it?"

"Yes, I do. It seems oddly familiar," I said.

"I heard the porters talking about it belonging to a house that had been forgotten, but you would appreciate them. I'm glad he was right. I'm Aggie," she offered. "Anything you need here, you ask for Aggie. I'm to help you in whatever way I can. And don't mind the Lady. She's an odd sort, but she's harmless. I think her hearts in the right place."

I thanked Aggie again and upon her departure, I sat on my bed, took a piece of ham and started to cry. I did not know then why the furnishings brought me such comfort or why exactly they moved me to tears. It was only years later after Judge Long passed that I came to learn the furniture belonged to my parents and was brought from their house to here. He hoped in some small way, he could help me recover what was forgotten and lost behind the cold convent walls.

Chapter 12

The days with the Longs passed quickly and were orchestrated with military precision. Each hour of the day held for itself a specific task, and I fell into the rhythm quite naturally having lived in the convent. Judge Long would leave at sunrise with a carriage awaiting him in the courtyard. He would tend to various legal matters and his holdings but would return at sunset, in time for supper.

Since Lady Isabella had claimed the dining hall for what she expected to be a gallery of my paintings in her honor, a smaller dining table was placed in what was originally intended to be a lady's recreational room. I would dress and eat my meals with them, while Frederick would share a variety of tales of his day that could be as delightful as retrieving a frightened cat in a tree to as horrifying as condemning a man to death by hanging. He took the horrifying incredibly hard, always muttering that he had no choice in the matter.

Subsequently, my days were left to Lady Isabella to claim. They were also in a pattern that I could anticipate. In the later part of the morning when the lighting was better, in her estimation, we would move to the great hall, where she had a fainting couch placed, and I was to sketch her. She thought it best I work with charcoal and pencils before she could decide what position she favored best and would therefore invest in paints. This dreariness would last hours until lunch was served.

On the days Lady Isabella was exceptionally tired, she would nap in what I can only suppose was originally intended to serve as the sitting room but now was an amalgamation of oddly shaped settees with various ornamentations. I would take my leave then and either walk about the property or read the books I had brought with me from the convent. It struck me peculiarly that in a house as large as this, and given Judge Long's profession, there was not a proper library or a study. I can only venture to guess that at one point there was, but it was overtaken by the Lady's eccentricities and replaced with either sculptures or vases or anything else that caught her fancy. They seemed the oddest of pairs, the two of them, and I could never unravel what it was that drew them together and kept them bound to each other.

It was on one such afternoon when the Lady woke early from her slumber to find me staring at the black and white daguerreotypes placed in precious frames along the mantel.

"Oh, Mary!" She picked up her teacup as if no time had passed, remarking the tea had grown cold. She rang a bell to have a servant bring a warm pot. "Those are pictures of Frederick as a young man." She rose and stood behind me. "See here, there is Frederick. That tall fellow in the trousers and shirt and the shorter fellow desperately reaching with his arm around Frederick's shoulder is Thomas. They were childhood friends. Thomas became a solicitor."

"Who is that very young boy off there in the background, just staring at them in the torn knickerbockers? He looks like he's barely a toddler," I asked.

"Oh, that is the devil himself. That's John Fairmount."

"Madame, the post." It was one of the servants delivering an ivory card on a polished silver tray. How was I to know with its black ink, it possessed what was to become my entire future and the life I now live?

Holding the correspondence in her plump hand and opening it delicately, she remarked, "Well, it looks like the devil has invited us to a celebration of his marriage at what will probably be the most garish of New Years Eve's balls. I can't for the life of me imagine what senseless creature would marry John Fairmount." Placing the invitation back into the envelope, she turned to me. "Normally, I would have the good sense to decline, but you've never been to a gala, have you, Mary?"

"No, madam, I haven't."

"But if you were raised properly and not cast off as you were . . ."

I interrupted, "I was orphaned, Lady Isabella."

"Yes. I know. But . . . " And there, she stopped herself. "Well, you are here now, and we are going to go and introduce you to refinement, culture and society. All the better things in life you would have known, if we knew." When she rang the bell again, the servant reappeared. "Send word that I want my dressmaker to come tomorrow at noon to start on a gown for Mary. We have a New Year's gala to attend at the Fairmounts'."

After bowing, he left us.

The dressmaker assembled my attire swiftly. What started as a roll of maroon fabric with large white flowers became a flowing gown of Victorian style with a modest neckline that rested around my shoulders. In what seemed a mere wink of time, I was back in the carriage heading toward my destiny, heading toward Huntington House, the Fairmounts' estate.

We rounded a deep dark wood, and when it felt one could not see anything other than trees, Huntington House sprang up from the dark like a Grecian temple. It stood formidable, with white Doric columns stretching up toward the evening sky. A remarkable contrast from The Long's manor house and in my surprise and delight, I gasped.

The entire building was ablaze with lanterns and candles, and, as we approached, I heard the rhythmic pounding of music I had never heard before. It was the opposite of the calming hymns of the convent whose intent were to create an ethereal air, or the chamber music of violins and harpsicord the Lady would bring to the house on chosen Sundays as her attempt to introduce me to culture. No, these sounds were not intended to calm but rather to stimulate. It was a sound that penetrated the body in an effort to corrupt the soul.

As we disembarked from our carriage, my senses were overwhelmed. A dizziness overcame me as I placed my foot on the first stone step leading the way up to the entrance.

"Are you alright, Mary?" It was Frederick who caught me. I nodded.

"I felt light-headed is all," I offered. "I'm fine." But, in truth, I was not sure I was. I longed for the quietness of my room in the convent. That image flashed in my mind, in what I know now was a warning.

"It's this ridiculous noise they call music," Lady Isabella responded. "No doubt he smuggled these musicians in from some horrific foreign land, and now we must suffer them. Have heart, Mary. I will be here with you." And she patted my hand most gingerly.

The butler removed our coats, and I was thrust into a world of bright lights and white-coated waiters. Some passed through the crowds with trays of food while others carried silver trays of bubbling champagne. It was the Lady who spoke, "And here lies Sodom and Gomorrah."

We settled ourselves in a corner by large potted palm plants and strategically placed statues I can only assume were there for the affair. As every moment passed, I wished more and more to disappear into the tapestry or curtains. I imagined myself sprouting wings and flying away, out into the dark and to the moon. I had no appetite or desire to eat, meekly waving away the trays that came before me. As the Longs became more and more consumed with meeting the other guests, I was left to stand on my own, but ever so close by, so I could be introduced as their newly discovered artistic protégé.

I was lost in these thoughts when I saw most beautiful woman, I had ever seen come toward us on the arm of a younger man. He had chestnut hair and a gentle face. She had the air of an angel, so perfect was her figure and so confident her smile. I could almost swear she glowed, as if she were divinity before us, and I did not know if somehow, I had crossed into a different realm altogether, a different reality with demons, saints and mortals. But it was the young man's gaze, his gentle, beautiful gaze that helped me keep my sanity intact.

"Your Honor, my lady, may I present my nephew, Harold LaCroix," the angel spoke, and in turn, that man who stood next to her now, who was my anchor in this chaos, replied, "Please call me Harry."

"Indeed," was Lady Isabella's reply.

"I was just about to tell Harold that you are great patrons of the arts when he insisted on being introduced," the angel continued.

"And how precisely is he your nephew?" Lady Isabella challenged them both with her eyebrow raised.

"Now, Lady Isabella, I would almost think you were offending my sensibilities. He is my nephew precisely for all the reasons that people become nephews. He's the son of my sister—"

But that man, the one she had introduced as Harold, interrupted, "You are quite right in your question, uh, Lady Isabella. It seems Aunt Lois was quite a surprise as my mother was almost eighteen years her senior."

He smiled, tipping his glass, and I thought my heart would melt. I felt an incredible comfort in looking at his face. His hazel eyes were warm and his manner calming. He had a careful fluidity in his movements that could put the most onerous beast at ease. And his voice was gentle, without judgment, and humble. My feelings were unlike anything I experienced in the presence of Marco. Here I felt a stillness as if suspended above the clouds in tranquility.

And then I saw *him*. Staring at us. Staring at Harold, as if, if he willed it, Harold would vanish from the earth in a blast of flames. He had the same dark eyes resembling that toddler in the picture. That small wayward child who seemed unkept and discarded. But the child was grown now, no more tattered pantaloons, but refined black satin trousers with a small white pinstripe down either side. He wore a meticulously fitted black linen jacket with satin accents that seemed so smooth and soft, your hand would desire to brush against the fabric just to feel it. His face was handsome and dangerous, and his voice smooth as velvet. He had an all-consuming magnetism that could stop your heart if he so will it.

He interrupted addressing us all, "Lois has always been an angel. Once I saw Lois, I knew I would never be complete without her. And I am blessed to have her as my wife. Only a miracle could tame my wild heart." And with a devilish, entrancing smile, he bowed and kissed his wife's hand.

87

We all stared in amazement as the devil incarnate whisked the angel away to dance. As the dialogue between the Longs and Harold continued, I caught glimpses of words, words relating to artists and paintings and presumably me, but I could not help but stare at the Fairmounts, at John Fairmount in particular. He held within himself an extraordinary power that intrigued me. It is something I have never encountered before or since. He could bend the world to his whim. John Fairmount merely needed to think it, and say it, and the earth would bend to have it done as he commanded.

It was Lady's Isabella's mention of my name that brought me back into my reality. "Mary, do come here so I might present you to Mrs. Fairmount's nephew . . . "

"Harry," he said and smiled. And, once again, I fell into the safety of his gaze.

"We found poor Mary at St. Agnes, that lovely convent up the hill. There was an art exhibit in her honor, and when we learned that poor Mary had lost her sponsor and was to be cast out into the cold, we could not hear of it! Could we, Frederick?"

"Yes, quite right," Frederick responded, sipping champagne through his moustache and lacking any interest in what Lady Isabella was saying.

It was the look of sadness that passed Harry's face that made me say, "To be fair, I could have stayed in the convent if I were to take my vows."

"Awful!" Lady Isabella continued. "What a solemn and solitary life for a young woman! An orphan no less!"

But Lady Isabella's rant on my behalf was circumvented by the tapping of utensils on glasses. A toast by John Fairmount for his wife. Blinding light flashes from photographers who appeared from the shadows. And the thundering sound of fireworks on the lawn startled me. I have never heard such noise. I wrapped myself in a curtain leaning against a wall, overpowered by it all.

It was Harry's voice again that saved me. "Can I track down a waiter for you? You look flushed."

I shook my head. "No thank you. It's just a lot of excitement from the convent or living with the Longs for that matter."

"They mentioned you are an artist. What sort of art do you, uh, do? We never got that far in the conversation, as we had John's announcement. I mean, do you sculpt? Do you paint? Do you have a subject you like to paint? Fruit and flowers . . ."

The sound of Harry's voice made me smile. "I paint portraits mostly." He nodded. "I have painted landscapes," I offered eagerly for fear that he would vanish and find me dull, "but mostly, I prefer to paint people."

"Well, there are certainly many potential subjects here." He gestured at the now empty room, as all the guests had vanished to watch the fireworks.

I could not help but smile. "I'm not sure anyone here would want their portrait from me?"

But he quickly retorted, "Oh, now don't say that. I'm sure you're quite good. The Longs think so. Artist-in-residence and all."

"I don't think I belong there with the Longs," I said, looking at the floor. "I don't think I belong here either." Realizing I might have offended Harry, I stuttered, "N-not, uh, not that it's not a lovely party that your aunt has thrown. I-I don't know why I said that. I'm," and here I took a deep breath, wishing the curtains would swallow me whole, "I'm very sorry . . . "

But, gracious as always, Harry simply said, "Allow me to let you in on a little secret." He took a step closer, and for the first time, since Marco, I thought my heart would burst from its rapid beating. "I don't feel I belong here either. And you can always tell me whatever you like, and I will always keep it safe." He made a cross over his heart. "Scout's honor. I just come for the free food and drink."

I could not help but laugh. I stared at his face, and he smiled. If I close my eyes, I can still see his face upon our first meeting. That loveliness in his eyes. The gentle curl of his lips. The bashful way he would look down and put his hands in his trousers in a boyish, playful way. Whatever hardships may have come, I will always remember and reflect upon the simple joy of that moment of our first meeting.

The colorful shadows cast from the fireworks flashed across his cheeks, and I wished with all my heart that he would kiss me as Marco did. I wanted to feel the gentleness of his lips, the sensation of his fingertips down my arms.

No, I didn't belong with the Longs, or as a guest at a lavish ball given by the Fairmounts. I belonged out there, in the forest that surrounded Huntington House. Out there, things that did not belong went to die. I knew it was wrong to wish for death. It was wrong to live in grief. But the more Harry asked me about the convent and Sister Ann, the more I could not help but feel such tremendous remorse for all the things in thought and deed.

As Lady Isabella called me away, I could not help feeling that childlike pull to hold Harry's hand. To simply belong anywhere, any place. To be claimed. My entire life up until then people loved me through pity. No one had ever loved me enough to simply claim me.

Chapter 13

It was Aggie who woke me the next morning with the opening of the curtains. The Longs had decided to forego church, since the evening past at the Fairmounts' had brought us home as the sun was rising. Mr. Long justified our absence by claiming he saw the vicar inebriated and hunched over on a chair as we left to get our carriage. He concluded it would be highly unlikely that anyone would be there to unlock the church doors.

"Oh, tell me about the gala!" Aggie opened the last remaining curtain in my room as a ray of sunlight brushed my face. She had become my friend now. And although we behaved properly in front of the Longs, she was my confidant and companion.

I stretched my arms over my head. "What time is it, Aggie?"

"Almost noon, and the Longs are still in slumber. I heard the Lady snoring something fierce from her room. I doubt the old bags of bones will be moving about much. I think we'll be lucky if we get them down the stairs for supper. So, come *tell*!" She shook my arm as she sat at the edge of my bed. "Tell me!"

Sitting up, I rubbed my eyes, as Aggie fluffed a pillow and dutifully placed it behind my head, balancing her chin on her elbow all the while waiting patiently.

"Well," I began, "there was food and champagne and an awful amount of noise. There were photographers. I did meet this one young man . . ."

"No! No! Tell me about Mr. Fairmount!" she said in a whisper. "I have heard he is the most gorgeous thing that walks the earth!"

"Aggie!" I exclaimed.

"I heard he casts spells."

"Where did you hear that? The Longs?" I laughed.

"No. It's true. I have it on good account. What's he like? Do his eyes pierce your soul? I hear that he can look at a person and know exactly where they are weak. He can see your insecurities, your sins, your desires . . . he can see it all. Did you speak to him?"

The idea that my improprieties would be visible to Mr. Fairmount disturbed me. "No, I don't think so. I don't think he took much notice of me. He was more interested in Harry."

"Harry?"

"Yes." I shifted in my bed and pulled my knees up to wrap my arms around them. "Harry is Lois Fairmount's nephew. Lois Fairmount, the wife of Mr. Fairmount, is like no one I have ever seen in my life. I swear if she appeared in the convent, I would have fallen on my knees praying, thinking I had seen an angel." She regarded me then. "Harry," I continued, "has the loveliest hazel eyes and the kindest of voices. I could simply get lost in the sound of Harry talking. I felt safe in his voice."

I knew full well that Aggie was still interested in hearing about John Fairmount, and, releasing a deep sigh, I decided to indulge her. "Mr. Fairmount has piercing dark eyes. He is tall of stature. He was impeccably dressed. His dark hair gleamed from pomade with only one rogue strand hanging over his eyes that sparkled with amusement."

"I bet he put it there on purpose," Aggie said, "to beguile. Go on!"

"I don't have much else on Mr. Fairmount, I'm afraid. He danced with his wife. He seems quite taken with her."

"No. No, I feel there is going to be more," Aggie offered. "I just feel it in my bones, Mary. I feel there is going to be more in your life of Mr. Fairmount."

I laughed nervously.

"He can crawl under your skin, that one can."

"I'd rather his nephew crawl," I said. Hitting me with a small pillow, Aggie rose to leave.

"I hope you see Harry again. He seems to have made your heart happy but mark my words on Mr. Fairmount."

And with that, Aggie left me to partake in the breakfast she left on my dresser and contemplate the new year that was to unfold.

I found myself thinking randomly of Harry in the weeks that followed, even more so when I learned of an upcoming dinner, we were all to attend the Fairmounts' weeks after the gala. This put the Longs in an even worse temperament as they dared not refuse, though they would have preferred to distance themselves from John Fairmount.

At times, I would lose myself reflecting on the sound of Harry's voice, which I had dutifully memorized. I would imagine him sitting next to me and talking to me in my room as the night would close in around me. He was my first thought in the morning and my last thought before I drifted off to sleep. He was my constant diversion to the monotonous nature of living with the Longs. He was my reprieve from my grief.

"I need more paint, Lady Isabella," I said one day as she sat in her repose, and I hid behind a canvas. She approved of my sketches for this particular study, and we had moved on to my applying paints to bring it to life. "I need more blue paint, specifically."

"Can't you mix a blue?"

"Actually, no. Blue is what is called a primary color. Along with yellow and red. It's what we use to create all colors," I said, putting down my brush. "I think, until I get more blue paint, that's about all I can do, Lady Isabella."

Here she sat up with her heavy bosoms falling on her knees. "I'm very disappointed, Mary." She looked as if she might cry as I crossed the room and retrieved her oriental silk robe. Wrapping it around herself, she continued, "I wanted to have this portrait for Frederick's birthday. It's coming up so rather quickly!"

"Where did you get the paint that I have now? I would like to go and pick my own."

"Absolutely out of the question! I will not have you in and out of shops like some commoner. You are a Whitcombe. You should have people for that sort of thing."

"It's fine, Lady Isabella. No one knows I'm a Whitcombe, and certainly no one will know in the shop," I tried to offer reassuringly.

"You are here to learn refinement and to scrub away all that rudimentary living from the convent. The manner in which you were hidden away fills me with rage! Absolutely unacceptable! I have told Frederick of my complete and utter . . . " but she was so flummoxed, she could not continue.

"It's fine, Lady Isabella." Taking her hand, I patted it, and brought her over to the drawing room, where I could ring the bell for tea. She had become more and more this way since the New Year's gala at the Fairmounts'. She was more inclined to have outbursts and then forget what made her angry.

It was Aggie who offered an explanation as I hid in the kitchen while Lady Isabella napped in her chair. "It's that Mr. Fairmount, I'm telling you. He cast one of his spells on her."

"Stop it, Aggie. There are no such things as spells."

"You might not be a believer now, Mary. But I'm telling you, there is an order to the universe. There's a push and a pull, and some people have the ability to alter it."

"I think you're reading too many of those strange books you hide under your covers."

"No. No, my grandmother," she lowered her voice and said almost in a whisper, "she knew of people who could do what Mr. Fairmount does. Thems were gypsies."

Changing the subject, I asked, "When are you next going into town? I need to pick out my own paints."

"Oh, the ones we got don't suit?" she asked.

"Just let me know when you go next, and I'll come with you. In all the time I've been here, I've never been allowed into town, and I would very much like to see it."

"Oh, the Lady won't like that."

"Well, we certainly don't have to tell her."

It was about a week later that I wrapped my coat tightly and ventured out with Aggie and the cook into town. They would leave early, as soon as Mr. Long had departed. It was a strange combination of walking and rides hitched on the back of hay bales, all impeccably timed. I could not contain my excitement for being out in the world.

I was always kept safely behind walls. The walls of the convent and now the walls of the Longs' estate. The smells of earth and man, all mixed together as the wagon brought us into the center of town. They were intoxicating. I was an innocent cast out to the world's inequities.

We all disembarked from the back of the trailer, and, after running to the front of the pull, Aggie climbed up and kissed the young coachman on the cheek. "Be back in two hours, love, and good luck!"

Hurrying back, she came to me.

"Alright, we have our work to do here, but mind to meet us at this exact spot in two hours. Look at your clock so you don't get it wrong. We'll need to be leaving then, and believe me when I tell you, the rest of them will leave you behind." Then, pointing off to the left, she said, "That's the paint shop. Be careful!" In the blink of an eye, she ran off.

It's amazing how Providence works. For how was I to know that, as I entered the shop door and heard the ringing of the bell, there I would see Harry, standing in front of the counter? He turned and saw me at once. His eyes were warm, and his face lit up—the same way Marco's would light up. There he was. Harry LaCroix, asking me why I was there, and handing me a small package of paints. He said delighted, "Here, these are for you."

I fought back the tears. The last gift of any form I received was from Marco.

"It's a brush and some paint powders. I thought you might like it." Noticing I wiped a tear, he quickly added, "You don't like it? You think I'm being forward?"

Shaking my head, I said, "It's perfect. I am grateful. Thank you." I turned the package over in my hands.

"I picked mostly the primaries," he said. "There are a few shades of blue. I favor blue."

I smiled.

"By some chance, would you have time for a small meal next door?"

It was a bar and grill with clean linens that served sandwiches, and we were escorted to a table by the window. This was the first time I ever sat and ate in an establishment. I let Harry request my meal, as I had no thoughts of protocol.

I tried with all my efforts to simply stare at Harry's face and try to avoid any nervous tendencies or any awkwardness that I might display. He asked about my stay at the Longs' and why I was there. It was an odd question, certainly one I had asked myself many times. I could not offer any other intelligent response other than to say I was there to paint the portrait of Lady Isabella.

I decided to direct our conversation to the paint powders. "How did you pick them?"

And here, Harry smiled. Oh, that smile warmed my heart. If I could spend the rest of my days coaxing a smile from Harry's lips, I would gladly do it.

"Well," he wiped his face with the cloth napkin, and, after swallowing, he said, "I picked the blue shades of powders that reminded me of the oceans I've traveled. There's a lovely deep blue that reminds me of the Mediterranean. And there's another beautiful blue with a slight green that remind me of the waters in Africa."

"Were you there long? In Africa?" I interrupted.

"I was there longer than I wanted." He looked down at the table. "The war was longer that any of us wanted."

"Do you ever wish to go back?" I asked.

"To Africa?" he asked. "No. No, there are too many ghosts for me there. I would much rather settle here with Aunt Lois and spend my days away, hunched over an oil lamp and wonderful dusty books, and, of course, dining with you, Mary."

I laughed.

"In truth," he added, "I do find much comfort in books, and it is good to be able to see Aunt Lois, but so far, the best part of it, is seeing you." He raised his glass to sip from it, and I could feel myself blush as I looked down at my fingers.

I offered what I could of my life with the Longs. The more I spoke to Harry, the more I came to realize that, in time, I would need to leave the Longs. There was so much I did not know about the world. I didn't know where I would go, or what I would do. As I shared these thoughts, Harry grew more and more apprehensive. His concern troubled me, for, outside of the sisters, very few worried about me at all.

I started to twist my fingers, a habit I developed after Marco's passing. Concluding my tale, I said, "The art exhibit was to raise funds so I could manage a small amount to venture into my own life. The sisters were very generous. So, you see, at some point, I do really need to go." I wasn't sure in saying the words out loud if I was trying to convince myself or Harry. I continued, "My father was William Whitcombe of lower Sussex County, and my mother was Grace."

It was here that Harry's face contorted. "You said 'William Whitcombe,' but you cannot mean the same one I think of. There were no survivors of the Whitcombe family that come to my mind."

"If you are thinking of the Whitcombes who came to their tragic death on a ship bound for New York, then we speak of the same. And there *were* survivors. There is me. I'm told I was too little to go with them on their journey. I had a sister once, but I don't really remember her."

"I don't understand." And here, Harry looked at me as if I were the most ridiculous person in the entire world.

"I lived. They died," I said plainly.

"I don't understand," he repeated. "Tell me, what became of your parents' fortune? Who brought you to the convent? Who is in possession of your father's estate? Do you know who might have his last will and testament?"

Harry proceeded with questions, and I could feel my heart sinking deeper and deeper. I felt a better companion when he thought nothing more of me than the poor orphan artist who was taken in by the Longs. These questions reminded me too much of Marco and his inquiries before his death. I felt the room begin to spin, as old accusations came into my mind and accosted me.

"I am sure of nothing. I don't know about my fortune. If there was any sum left, the sisters would have given it to me. The money I received was from the sale of my paintings. I sold almost all of them," I said simply.

"Mary." He placed his hand over mine, and I could feel the warmth of his skin. My breath quickened and an uneasiness rose in my chest. "If what you say is true, if you are an heiress, you don't need to run and hide, you could simply claim—"

But I could not bear it any longer. I could hear Mother Superior's admonishment for all that happened with Marco and Sister Ann. It was a curse. Being a Whitcombe was a curse.

No one would ever know me as anything other than a wretched heiress who was orphaned. Staring at the lady's clock that hung around my neck, I announced, "I must be getting back. They're waiting for me. We all agreed to meet and journey back."

Seeing the distress on his face, I could not help but say, "Don't worry, Harry. Something will come up. Just pray for me, Harry. As Sister Ann would always say, just pray, and God will answer you." Gathering my things as Harry rose, I hurried out the door and did not look back.

Chapter 14

From the moment I shared it with Harry, the seed of leaving the Longs was planted firmly in my mind. Each day it grew deeper roots. I was no longer interested in entertaining the whims of Lady Isabella, finding them constraining. The presence of Judge Long and his stories of propriety irritated me.

"She's not the same, Frederick," I would hear her whisper to Judge Long at night when they thought I was buried in a book in the far corners of the foyer.

And his hushed response, "It's just part of her adjustment"

In the evenings, I would pretend to sleep as I would hear the creaking of my bedroom door open. Judge Long would take one step into my room and stare. Just stare as if contemplating a ghost from his past.

I started to lock the door. It was claustrophobia fostered by Lady Isabella's hysteria and Judge Long's desire to appease his wife that I knew my time was coming close. I prayed that something, anything, would give me a sign of where I was to go next.

They often say to be grateful for unanswered prayers, and I would have wished with all my heart it was so. But no. My prayer was to be answered on an overcast morning as I walked along the gray stonewall that surrounded the barren manor. Anything living knew, there would be no joy within. But on the other side of the dirt road away from the confinement, there were tall grasses, small flowers, and, on occasion, a butterfly. These walks gave me the courage to imagine something different. Something different than the repetitive nature of life with the Longs.

It was a distant sound at first, something entirely unfamiliar. Mechanical. Not the sound of the horse and carriages that normally would come by and disturb gravel and stones. The sounds came from a distance behind me. I was compelled to stop and await whatever fate was to find me.

Placing my hand over my forehead to shade the sun, I saw a motor car. Something quite rare to behold. It was black, long and thin without a top, and a shiny silver around the sides. In the front of the motor car were bright lights that seemed to me to be oddly shaped eyes surrounding a shining grill that I fancied was an unusually placed mouth grinning maniacally. I stood there, curious by what was getting closer and closer to me until I could make out a figure behind the wheel—a man with dark hair and a dark coat. It was none other than John Fairmount!

"Mary!" he yelled cheerfully as his motor car came to a stop before me. "I thought I'd find you here. It is Mary, isn't it?"

"Yes," I answered.

"You came to my New Year's Eve gala, did you not? The artist-in-residence with the Longs?"

"Yes." I repeated.

"You didn't enjoy the music, did you, Mary?

Furrowling my brow, I asked, "Pardon?"

"I didn't see you dance. But I did note that you spent time with my wife's nephew, Harry."

He studied me now.

"Hop in, Mary. I have something to show you," he said with a lilt to his voice.

I shook my head, not fully comprehending.

"Come into the car, Mary," his tone changed to one of authority. He swung the passenger door open.

I shook my head again. "No, thank you, Mr. Fairmount. I'd rather not."

And here, he smiled so wide, and there was a spark in his eye, as if something new had ignited within him. Leaning back into his seat, he rested his arm on his lap and laughed. "Mary, I swear to all that you hold holy, I will conduct myself in a most gentlemanly manner. I have something to show you that I think you should see. It might be of some importance to you and Harry."

"Harry?" I asked, bewildered.

"Yes. Harry," he said cheerfully, no longer looking at me but out in the distance at the road ahead. He tapped his fingers on the car door with his arm resting on it, the passenger side door waiting; open before me.

He said nothing further. His gazed fixed on the horizon ahead. He began to hum, waiting patiently.

I don't remember how it happened, or how my legs found their way into Mr. Fairmount's car. It was as if he made them move without my knowledge or control. It was the slamming sound of the car door that awoke me out of whatever daydream I was in.

Finally turning to me, he said, "Good girl, Mary," as he drove off.

The drive seemed longer than I had expected. At first, I could not place the roads that unfolded before us. A panic began to grip me. "Mr. Fairmount, I fear the Longs will be looking for me. It might be best if we turn around."

"No one is looking for you, Mary," he said, and a chill went up my spine. I gripped the motorcar's door handle. I contemplated the speed and if I could survive expulsion. "I had the woman who brings her tea drop a sedative in her cup. She'll be unconscious for a while. Plenty of time for me to show you what I'd like you to see." He must have sensed my fright, as he gently added, "No harm will come to her, Mary. I assure you."

We drove through hills and valleys, passing beautiful cottages and lovely little villages, and Mr. Fairmount would wave and honk his horn, and all would come to greet him. No one was concerned, nor took notice of me. It was when we started to drive in a steady incline that something in my heart stirred. A strange familiarity took me over, and I could not help but feel an eagerness in my soul.

We drove, and I seemed well acquainted with small parcels of dirt long forgotten in the recesses of my mind. I could anticipate the expected foliage or boulder in the next turn. He slowed down now, signaling the near end of our exploit passing wild roses and iron fencing.

When we stopped at an iron gate with a large "W" intertwined within the bars, I felt an inexplicable and overwhelming urge to weep. Mr. Fairmount opened my door and instructed me to disembark. Like an automaton, I obeyed. Lighting a cigarette, he leaned against the motorcar and waited for my reaction.

"Does this look at all familiar to you, Mary?" he asked.

"I don't know." I traced the iron W with my fingers. Through the bars, I could see an overgrown fountain and hedges long abandoned.

"This was your home, Mary," Mr. Fairmount said, pointing with his cigarette. "This is where you grew up, until you were dropped off at the convent. This is your estate."

Placing my head on the metal bars, the painful memory of when I left was brought to my conscious mind. Without my consent, I relived that fateful day, a memory long buried and forgotten now in horrid, vivid detail. I started to sob, gripping the bars.

As Mr. Fairmount walked up behind me, I whimpered. His presence began to confuse my senses. I found it difficult to breathe. "This can be yours again, Mary. I could get this for you."

"I don't understand." I muttered gasping for air, clinging to the metal bars for dear life.

He took a step closer. His presence all-encompassing now. "You can do something for me that no one else can, Mary. Harry has been quite taken with you. He talks often of you to Lois."

I could feel myself blush. He took one more step closer, his warm breath landing on the back of my neck.

Leaning in he whispered into my ear now, "You have feelings for Harry, don't you, Mary?" I swallowed hard.

"You see . . . ," I could feel his warm breath on my cheek as he came closer, his words intoxicating, his tone seductive, "I promised Lois I would help you . . . *leave the Longs* . . ." Having said those last three words, he retreated and waited for me to turn and face him.

I regained my composure. I found him leaning on his car again. Watching me. Studying me as if I were prey.

"You see, Mary," he resumed in a calm confident tone, "my nephew Harry is spending more time with his dear aunt—my wife—than I think suits. And I would like you to help me limit their time together. And, in turn, I will give you this."

I laughed. "How do you know I'm a Whitcombe? Did Harry tell you?"

He did not reply.

"How in the world can you give me my own home? I have no papers. No will and testament." His spell broken, my senses regained, I added, "I think it's time you drive me back to the Longs."

"You doubt me," Mr. Fairmount said pleased. "Hold out your hand."

"No," I protested. "I've had quite enough of this adventure. Please return me home."

"I have returned you home," he said amused. "It was you who prayed to leave the Longs, did you not?"

How did he know the contents of my prayers? He walked towards me again, his gaze never leaving my eyes forcing me to not look away. He placed a small item which appeared involuntarily in my cupped hand. "Do you know what that is, Mary?"

I was again transfixed, staring into the cool dark abyss of his eyes.

"Marco gave you that medallion, did he not? You lost it the day you almost drowned," he said matter-of-factly. Looking away, he released his hold on me again.

I grabbed the metal bar with my free hand to prevent me from falling. Old ghosts were visiting me now from all directions. I looked down at my hand and there it was, the medallion of the Virgin Mary. In my head I heard Marco's voice whisper, "My Mary."

"You seem more convinced now." Reaching into his pocket, he pulled out another cigarette and tapped it on his gold engraved case. "My wife will be granting me an heir soon. She'll need a governess. That will be you. You will come to live with us at Huntington House. You will keep Harry

LaCroix occupied by your attention. How you manage that will be your concern, not mine."

Words finally returned to me now. "How did you . . . How do you know about Marco?"

But John Fairmount did not answer. His expectations clearly articulated now, he simply stated, "Your fortune in exchange for my nephew. Your choice."

I nodded in agreement.

"No," he hissed. "I need you to say it. I need you to say it out loud." A long pause passed between us.

"I will keep your nephew occupied and away from your wife in exchange for my fortune." A loud crash of thunder sounded, and a bright light flashed in the sky. The heavens heard me and replied.

"It will rain soon. I should get you back," was Mr. Fairmount's joyful response.

Chapter 15

In retrospect, I should have felt more guilt for leaving the Longs and Aggie behind, and most certainly for the way it was carried out. It was a covert operation that Mr. Fairmount handled with much ease. I was to simply attend dinner with the Longs that Mr. Fairmount arranged after his gala, and everything else was to be left to him. The instructions were delivered to me by Mr. Gross, Mr. Fairmount's valet during one of my walks. I was to communicate with no one until the time came.

I felt an overwhelming sense of anticipation and relief that I would be leaving my current captors, as I came to regard them. At the time, I did not see them as the careful attending guardians they so hoped to be. It is only now that I look back and see that all their efforts, all of Lady Isabella's peculiar behaviors and attempts to restrict my access were simply because they knew I was not prepared for the world. They most certainly knew I was not prepared for John Fairmount. Even Aggie knew I was no match for him. Somewhere deep inside, I must have known the same, for I even kept my leaving from her.

This is the inevitable folly of youth. It is a folly to condemn those who desperately try to protect us and steer us away from harm, to deem them wardens in our rebellious attempt to claim independence and freedom when incapable of handling either ourselves. Both gained without a foundation will always lead to disaster, as was the case with me.

I can still picture the look of shock and betrayal on Lady Isabella's face, and the look of resolute sadness on Judge Long's. I have that image embedded in my mind forever.

It was before they departed that John Fairmount announced, "Before we end our evening, I want to share a bit of good news with all of you. Lois will you join me darling? She came and stood by John, and grabbing both her hands he said, "My darling Lois, whom I will never deserve will be providing me with an heir." Dropping to both knees like a servant, he kissed her hands. "You are the only angel who has ever and will ever grace my life."

And there it was the heavenly comedy played out in full form, the devil and the angel in harmony. Lois begged him to stand, and it was Lady Isabella who broke the awkwardness of the moment. "Many blessings," she muttered. "Come, Mary."

John released Lois's hands, and addressed Lady Isabella while he helped her with her coat, "Oh, yes. I should mention that since Lois is carrying our child, I will require a nursemaid to care for her and the child. We are very fortunate, as Mary has so graciously agreed to serve in this endeavor."

"Impossible!" Lady Isabella shouted, recoiling from John's assistance. "Mary is *my* ward and she belongs with us! Frederick do something!"

"Lady Isabella!" Mr. Fairmount scolded. "Mary is a grown woman. I made an offer and she accepted. You can't compel her to come with you."

"She doesn't even have her things!"

John interrupted her, "Actually everything that Mary owns was placed in the nursery wing during dinner."

It was Judge Long now who answered, "How in the world did you manage that?"

But Mr. Fairmount smiled wildly. "Mr. Gross, my valet arranged them."

It was over. There was nothing more to say. And I, with what I can only assume resembled that of childlike triumph, was escorted up the large winding staircase by John Fairmount and out of their sight for the last time.

He walked me to the far hall, guiding me along with his hand on the middle of my back, and I like a marionette, responding to the pressure of his fingertips, knowing when to turn and when to stop, all the while in awe of the carvings on the walls and ceiling and delicate iron work around lamps and lanterns.

"Here we are, Mary," he said in the most delightful tone. "This is your room. I picked it out myself."

Opening the door, I could not help but be overwhelmed by the size and beauty of it all. It was considerably larger than my room with the Longs. There were four windows that stretched from ceiling to floor with boxed seats that were equally situated along the wall directly from the door. On each window seat were pink satin pillows and others in ivory linen with delicately embroidered flowers in green, purple, blue and rose silk thread.

The walls had mahogany wainscoting and a dark green wallpaper with small flecks of gold that sparkled in the sunlight. The ceiling had thick beams that crossed in patterns and contained within them delicate carvings of flowers and angels. In the middle, as they met, hung a tremendous gaslit chandelier in a gold tone with tiny pink and white crystals that fell and cast small prisms of light around the room.

To the right was a beautifully carved mahogany bed, and on the bed was the loveliest soft satin bedcover with oriental flowers in the same color scheme and pattern. On the middle of the bed, to my astonishment, was the thing I had not seen in years, the thing I had left behind in my childhood, the thing Uncle Thomas promised but never brought to me: my rag-clothed bunny, no more tormented than before time had passed. I embraced my doll and slowly started to weep.

Mr. Fairmount did not seem to notice, but walking toward the first window, he said, "Your room faces the garden and the fountain. It's a rose garden. I seem to recall you were fond of gardens."

Wiping the tears from my eyes, I said, "Yes. I love flowers. This is all quite lovely. I don't know how to repay you."

"Repay me?" John laughed. "Oh, no, Mary. This is a business arrangement. You deliver what I asked, and the rewards increase. This is just a sign of my good faith in the effort. Now, come here and look." I walked over obediently. "If you turn your neck, you can see in the solarium. That is the solarium my dear wife built for her nephew. It's their refuge. You can see when they are there together. You understand, Mary, I *do not* want them together." I nodded. "Then your employment begins at this moment. I suggest you find your way down and disperse their gathering."

"How would you like me to. . .?" I asked.

"Mary," John said simply, "you are a clever girl," as if there was nothing left to be said.

I nodded again in agreement as Mr. Fairmount left my room and closed the door.

After placing my stuffed rabbit on my bed, I navigated my way from my room and down the staircase in utter awe of the size and beauty of it all. I noted that the carpet on the steps was comprised of a beautiful red oriental weaving which, unlike the Longs' manor, made no sound as one pressed on the steps. Reaching the bottom and turning to my left, I passed Mr. Fairmount's study, and straight ahead was a glass door that fogged over. I heard muffled sounds as I turned the brass knob.

I caught them in mid-laughter. It was Lois who noticed me first. "Mary!" she said delighted. "Come join us."

"How are your accommodations?" Harry asked.

"They're breathtaking," I said, adding, "Thank you sincerely, Mrs. Fairmount, for your generosity."

"Oh, no, dear," Lois replied. "That was entirely John's doing. He spent the most meticulous care in setting your room. He even ordered that chandelier and bed linens from Paris. He spared no expense."

Wringing my fingers together in nervous manner, I said, "I don't know what to say exactly."

"Nothing at all, dear!" Lois said in a most cheerful tone, raising her eyebrow slightly. "I did sneak a peek. He has extraordinary taste, John does. I'm not sure I could have appointed the room better myself."

"Of course he has extraordinary taste," Harry replied. "He married you, Lois." And here they both smiled at each other, and I could see what it was that had unsettled Mr. Fairmount. They spoke to each other without needing words. There was an unusual understanding between them I had never encountered before or since. It was something celestial.

Remembering why I was sent, I looked at Harry and asked, "I've never really had a tour of the full grounds, and since I'll be living here now, would it be possible to see Huntington House?"

"Yes. Of course!" he replied, slightly embarrassed. "Of course. I'll get our coats. There's a brisk wind out there; don't let the sun setting fool you." After bowing to Lois with a wide smile, he departed.

"I absolutely adore my nephew," Lois said with a look of pride as she rose. "Be warned, Mary," she said with a lilt in her voice, "I never want to see Harry hurt. He is the one person on this earth I have sworn to keep happy."

"What about Mr. Fairmount? Didn't you swear to keep him happy?"

"No." And saying such, she left the room.

It was near dusk now as Harry led me down the stairs of the solarium into the garden. "I suppose you're eager to see everything, Mary," he said. "I would be the same way, although this is a better tour handled in the morning. I regret I won't be here to see you in the morning as I'm leaving tonight. But I hope that you'll be quite happy here."

Stopping at a particular vibrant red rose that showed even as the dusk approached, he said, "These here are Lois's favorite. John had them planted here specifically for her. If you look," here he turned and pointed to a window on the second floor, "out that window you can see them quite easily."

"Is that where you stay when you're here?" I asked.

"No." he said laughing, "no, I stay on the complete opposite side. That's Lois's room. It's for the best I'm not nearer. If I were, I would be tempted to tap morse code through the walls. We did that as children. Drove my grandparents mad."

"You must love your aunt very much," I said.

"I love her with all my soul, Mary," he said very seriously.

"Is there no room to love another?" I asked.

He grew quite solemn then, and, placing his hands in his coat pockets, he looked at me, blinking as the setting sun danced on his face. "We should head back. There won't be enough light for us to climb the steps into the manor, and I would not want you hurt. There will be a carriage for me soon."

We walked back toward the solarium. The sun cast thin shadows before us as if it knew of our impending doom.

Chapter 16

As the weather lightened, Harry and I took walks around the grounds and sat under trees to cool ourselves in the shade. He would read me poetry, and I would watch his lips move as he recited each sound. I would rest my head on his shoulder and close my eyes as his voice mixed with the sound of the trees.

On more than one occasion, I would drift off listening. Harry with his kind heart never took offense but would sit perfectly still until I stirred awake, always smiling down on me. These are my happy memories from that time in our lives. But always in my mind I wondered if there was room for any other love in Harry's heart, beyond his devotion to Lois.

Any warm feelings I felt for Harry were maligned by Mr. Fairmount's instructions and observations. His omnipresence always made me doubt if Harry's affections were genuine or the mere orchestration of convenience. At the end of every week, in the envelope with my wages was a carefully crafted note by Mr. Fairmount's hand. The messages were simple: *Well done this week, Mary.* Or *You can do better.* Or *Disappointing show.* The pendulum swing was unpredictable and my desire to be praised persistent.

I will confess, I did feel a tremendous fondness for Lois even though I fancied her my enemy and my rival in my quest for not only Harry's affection but also the Whitcombe estate. I could understand why others delighted in her presence. She had a quick mind and generous heart. I'm not sure if there was ever true malice in Lois, although she understood the emotion thoroughly. She had the most forgiving nature that I came to understand this was why she glowed. The purity of her soul cast her alongside angels and saints, which naturally put my own into sharp judgment.

"Do you know where I put the latest Walter Crane nursery papers?" Lois asked, moving a stack of books from one area to another in what was to become the heir Fairmount's room upon his birth.

It was a large room, sufficiently close to Lois's. John had installed an adjoining door, so that at any moment, Lois could enter. She insisted she was to be near her child at all points in time. To me, this would have typically been the role of the governess, or more specifically, my role. But having grown up with too many governesses in her lifetime, she insisted. It was supremely unorthodox, but Lois had her reasons, and no one saw fit to argue.

"I think we placed it over by that table by the lamp." I walked over there to find a large portfolio of various papers and brought it to her.

"Thank you, Mary!" she said, delighted. "The more this baby grows, the more I think my mind is shrinking. Do you know I spent an entire hour yesterday wondering where I put my pearls, when they were around my neck the entire time? It wasn't until I walked by a mirror that I saw them in my reflection."

"I suppose that happens. You have so much to think about," I offered.

"I'll tell you what I'd rather think about." She seated herself on a plush upholstered chair that was just delivered for the room. "I'd rather think about anything else entirely. What are you reading in the library? Is there anything missing you'd like me to have brought here?"

"No. Thank you. I just finished Shakespeare's sonnets with Harry," I said, starting to blush.

"Yes. He is quite a poetry aficionado, my nephew." I think she noticed me blush. "I don't wish to pry, Mary. I leave Harry to his privacy. Don't feel obliged to share your intimacies." She pulled an upholstered ottoman closer to rest her legs.

I pulled up a wooden stool and rested my arms on my knee. "What was Harry like as a child?"

"Oh, he was the most precious thing!" Lois smiled. "I remember when my sister brought him home. He was the tiniest baby. Such a good nature. He never fussed. I was seven years old, and I slept in his room on a mattress I had the butler put on the floor. Oh, my mother was so appalled. But I was relentless. I would not move. I would wake up randomly to make sure the baby was warm and comfortable. I even dismissed the governess." Here she smiled. "I didn't like the way she was holding him, and he would cry in her arms. He would not cry in mine."

"He's lucky to have you," I said, suddenly feeling melancholy.

"He wasn't always with me. My sister took him away, but in time, we came to spend the summers together." She paused and studied me then. "Mary, please don't think this harsh. I know you accepted this post to escape the Longs, but if at any point in time you feel the need to pursue something other than being my co-conspirator, as it were, in this decorating enterprise…" here she gestured to the room around us, "this nursery that may never be completed, know that I'd harbor no ill will toward you. If you wanted something else, I would understand."

"I'm quite happy here, Mrs. Fairmount."

Nodding in agreement, she reached out her hand. "Then let's look again at those papers." But before I could turn to get them, Mrs. Fairmount gasped and clutched her side.

"Are you alright, Mrs. Fairmount?" I asked.

Her breathing came more quickly, and I could see there was tremendous pain in her face, although she would not cry out. "Water?" I asked in exasperation. But she shook her head.

I ran down the stairs, shouting, "Find the doctor! Someone get the doctor!"

It was Mr. Fairmount who caught me at the bottom of the staircase. "What is this fuss?" He seemed disturbed.

"Mrs. Fairmount needs a doctor," I said in a panic.

Clutching me by the shoulders, he shouted, "Gross! Gross!" Gross appeared like an apparition from vapors. "Get the doctor now!" In a half bow, Gross was gone.

Mr. Fairmount cast me aside as he let go of my shoulders and flew up the stairs. I sat down hard on the steps. Arising, I followed and became witness to the most astonishing affair. The tempest of his temperament softened when he saw Mrs. Fairmount on the floor clutching the arm of her chair.

With the gentlest demeanor, he crouched down next to her and stroked her hair, whispering, "It will be fine, Lois."

She turned to look into his eyes and immediately her pain was relieved. He lifted her up gently and carried her to her room. She was mesmerized looking in his eyes while he repeated, "It will be fine, Lois. It will be fine, my angel."

By the time the doctor arrived, Mr. Fairmount had settled Lois well. Leaving the room as the doctor instructed, he closed the door behind him and proceeded to pace the long corridor. I felt a useless thing, a silly observer to the inner working of the Fairmounts. I waited, sitting on the top rung of the steps with my hands in my lap.

An hour later, the doctor finally emerged and cautiously said, "Mr. Fairmount, a word?"

I observed them, huddling in the dark corner of the corridor in hushed tones and with nodding heads. Having concluded his instructions, the doctor found his way to me, tipped his hat and proceeded down the staircase.

"Will she be alright?" I asked, standing slowly and smoothing out my dress.

He ran his fingers through his hair and let out the slowest breath. Finally placing his hands in his pockets, he answered, "Yes. I willed it so. See to it that she rests. She needs to rest. Place yourself in the chair by the window and see what she needs once she awakens."

I sat there perched like a bird while the sun set, too afraid to move. Lois finally stirred several hours after the dark had cast itself in the room, and only moonlight fell gently on her pillow.

"Harry . . . " she whispered.

"No, Mrs. Fairmount," I said, finally standing up from all that time sitting in the chair. "It is me. It's Mary. I've been sitting here waiting for you to awaken."

"Will you please find Harry for me?" she asked with a weak, sleepy tone.

"I cannot, Mrs. Fairmount. It's late. He's gone back to the city. Perhaps you'd like something to eat? Or perhaps you'd like something to drink? I can get that for you." Bending over, I lit her oil lamp by her bed, and it illuminated the room. "How are you feeling?"

"Disoriented," she confessed.

"The doctor said you'll be alright. You just need to rest," I said encouragingly.

"Some soup if you don't mind, Mary."

I poured her a glass of water and left. I walked down the large staircase to the main entrance and then to the kitchen where the cook, who had long gone to bed, left a pot of chicken soup warming on the stove. Finding a bowl, I dipped the ladle into the warm broth.

"She's hungry; that's a good sign." The voice startled me, and I nearly fell into the pot. It was Gross.

"Good Lord! Don't you sleep? You just lurk about, don't you?" I said, irritated.

Turning the switch to light the gas lantern on the wall, he said, "I do as Mr. Fairmount wishes, much like you do, Miss Whitcombe."

"What did he have you do, just sit here looking after the pot?" I asked, annoyed again, as I filled the bowl, placed it on the table and looked for a spoon.

He handed me a silver spoon and a cloth napkin. "No. I'm to look after you, and ensure you do as Mr. Fairmount asks."

"What do you know about me and Mr. Fairmount?" I asked, horrified.

"Everything Mr. Fairmount knows, I know, Miss Whitcombe." He stood up to leave the room but turned to give me his counsel. "As one servant to another, if I were you, I would persuade Harry LaCroix to marry me in earnest and leave. That might be a better ambition than securing your fortune. Fortunes can disappear, can't they? It would allow you to permanently secure your full future. I would do it swiftly before Mr. LaCroix were ever to discover your arrangement with Mr. Fairmount. He might come to conclude that your feelings were never genuine, and he was just a pawn in a jealous game to secure your wealth. These things always find a way of leaking out." After turning the hourglass on the counter over so the sand would spill through to the other side, he disappeared into the darkness.

Lois ate most of her meal. I helped her dress into her nightgown and left the room so she could sleep. It was several hours past midnight when I entered my room to see the bright red glow of a cigarette light up in the darkness, piercing it with an ominous glow.

I fumbled in the dark and lit the oil lamp on my dresser by the door. I could see him better now. "Did she ask for Harry?"

"Yes, Mr. Fairmount."

"Did she ask for me?"

"No, Mr. Fairmount."

Mr. Fairmount blew out little circles of smoke. He studied me then, seated in my vanity chair, with one leg crossed over the other. His shoes were shining. His garments, immaculate.

"How long have you been living here now, Mary?" he asked.

"Two seasons. A little more."

"Has my nephew asked for your hand, Mary?"

"No, Mr. Fairmount." I leaned against the door, holding the knob in both my hands behind me. He changed his gaze to the side of the room with the view of the solarium, as if he were studying the empty air. Sitting back most comfortably, he smoked his cigarette.

After a while he spoke again, "Mary, I left your baptismal records on the dressing table behind me. The next thing I will get for you is the will," he said matter-of-factly. After a time, he added, "Did you know that Harry was trying to find your fortune?"

"No." There was a long pause. "He asked me about it. I never knew he tried."

"He failed," Mr. Fairmount said. "If he brings it up again, dissuade him. I can't have my good-natured nephew muddling my affairs. You understand that don't you, Mary?" Here he finally looked at me again, his eyes piercing my soul. "Those who are pure of heart sometimes lack the ability to do what's necessary to secure success. They let their conscience dictate their actions. But you don't struggle with your conscience, do you, Mary?"

He stood up now and put out his cigarette on a tray by my vanity.

"Do you ever wonder, Mary, after all this time, if Harry comes here to see you or Lois?"

"I would imagine both, Mr. Fairmount."

He smiled. "I would imagine he would still come to see Lois even if you weren't here. But I'm not sure if he would visit, were it reversed. Are you sure, Mary?"

I stepped aside from the door, and Mr. Fairmount left me alone with my thoughts.

Chapter 17

I would like very much to erase what happened in the time that followed forever from my memory. But it cannot be so. For my actions changed the lives of many, many who I came to love over time.

I would like to say it was my inexperience with life, or perhaps the alluring nature of temptation. Perhaps it was simply a desire to finally control something that was mine. I did not intend to harm anyone. But I was without roots.

I so desperately wanted to be saved. Saved by anyone who wanted me in whatever form that could take. I was not discerning. I was insecure, desperate and lonely.

I lived under the watchful eye of Mr. Gross, trading what I perceived to be a prison with the Longs for another. Gross knew where I went, when I returned. He knew if Harry was with me or not. I often wonder if he knew what we said when we were together.

In those two seasons I stayed with The Fairmounts, Harry and I had talked of a future in passing. But it was never secure.

It was never clear. He was always more concerned about Lois and his nephew-to-be.

I ceased to see that spark in his eye when he saw me. Or the bashful way, he would look at his shoes when embarrassed. I became a fixture, the comfortable chair one might sit in after a long day, regarding it more for its usefulness rather than any desire for it in particular. It was as if any chair would suffice as long it filled the obligation.

It was seeing Harry sitting quietly in a chair in her bedroom, staring out the window to the garden, waiting for Lois to awaken, that stirred me. It was a vexation. One that I had not known before or since. He did not tell me he was going to come. And, in the last few weeks, he had become distant. I feared I could not hold his attention or perhaps worse that he knew of my agreement with his uncle.

I was no longer sure of Harry's affections, nor of my ability to maintain them. All this time, I thought Harry and I would be together, and much like Marco desired, would live from my fortune. I would give it to him without his assistance so he would be safe, and nothing would befall him for seeking it. But here, I was confronted with the possibility that Harry would no longer desire me, and my fantasy was premature and ill-conceived. It was a fear that loomed over my head and became an integral part of my being then.

"Harry!" my scolding was masked in a whisper as I opened her door. "What are you doing here? You never told me you were coming."

Turning, he smiled at me. Then he rose and walked toward me, motioning for me to step out into the hallway. "Well, I came to see Lois," he said as I closed her door behind us. His hands were in his pockets, and he rocked back and forth on his heels like a schoolboy. His tone asserted it was the most obvious answer and how silly I was to even ask.

"She needs her rest," I said, perturbed. "It's not appropriate for you to enter her bed chambers. What if Mr. Fairmount saw you, or his valet?"

"Gross?" Harry laughed. "What do I care if they do? I'm sure they have seen me in her room before." And here he stopped rocking as the light in his face dimmed.

I twisted my fingers together, desperately trying to calm myself as I paced. "It's not appropriate."

"Mary," here he took a deep breath and paused, "she is my aunt. My only family. I will determine what is appropriate and what is not."

Seeing the stern look on his face, I reluctantly nodded in agreement as he turned and re-entered her room. I stood outside Lois's bedroom door frozen. That was it, wasn't it? I had come this far. Perhaps it was time to take whatever documents Mr. Fairmount had provided and leave. I had saved my wages. No one would miss me. No one would care.

I would reach out to Aggie, and she would help me. She would forgive me for my sudden departure. She would tell me where to go. This was how my mind justified itself as I stood, my head down and fists clenched, leaning against Lois's bedroom door.

It was the sound of Mr. Fairmount's steady steps ascending the stairs which caused me to reenter Lois's room. I could not risk him finding Harry there alone and me failing to keep them apart. At least not until I was certain of what I wanted. Lois had awoken at this point with Harry standing near her, his arms folded, smiling. Mr. Fairmount entered. "Lois my, darling." He beamed with large, blooming, red roses in his arms, and, seeing that she was not alone, he said steadily, "It seems we all have come to cheer you, my love." Placing the roses in a crystal vase in the nightstand by the door, he continued, "I trust you are improving, given the visitors here."

"They're beautiful, John. Thank you." Then she addressed Harry and me, "John had the rose bushes brought here from France and planted for me. He knew I loved them. Harry, walk Mary through the garden and point these out. They're over by the fountains."

"I will hold no ill will if you were to assemble a bouquet for Mary," Mr. Fairmount said pointedly.

Forcing a smile, Harry escorted me out of Lois's room for the second time.

The sun was warm, although there was an unusual quiet. Our footsteps seemed louder somehow as we strolled the grounds. "I'm sorry, Harry," I said. "I shouldn't have admonished you."

"I completely understand, Mary. You care for Lois. You thought I disturbed her rest."

"Yes," I said weakly, knowing full well it was a lie. It was not any concern I had for Lois, but rather the distance that had grown between Harry and myself that concerned me.

Words ceased in our throats. There was no longer talk of our future, or of parcels of land, or of cottages. He did not ask me about my art, nor if I had need for any more paint powders. I was lost in the melancholy nature of my thoughts when I heard Harry say, "So it seems we reached the end."

I stared at him in disbelief. Utterly lost.

He must have noted my expression, for he quickly added, "The end of the garden. See, the hedges are up ahead. Should we turn back?"

He saw a small tear escape my cheek. "Mary," he asked in concern, "what is wrong?"

I shook my head slowly. "Nothing. Nothing is wrong, Harry."

Placing his arm around my shoulders, he guided me back to Huntington House. This was the first form of affection

Harry had displayed since our courtship in the spring. Oh, how I missed his affections.

Harry retired to his room, and I to mine. Sitting in front my vanity, I stared at my reflection for a while and then at my hands. I had in my possession my baptismal records and my certificate of birth. I did not have the will.

I closed my eyes, for how long I do not know, but I opened them to find Mr. Fairmount standing behind me. Like a ghost, he entered my room, without any sound.

"You look melancholy, Mary," he said.

I regarded him in the mirror. "I am."

"Did Harry mention his intended arrival today?" he asked.

"No." I responded truthfully.

He nodded. "Do you think he still longs for you? Thinks of you when he sleeps?"

"I don't know."

He nodded again. "Do you miss it, Mary? Knowing that you were the singular thought in a man's mind?"

I swallowed hard. And there it was, implanted in my mind, the image of Marco and I together. All those thoughts, sensations, bated breath . . . I closed my eyes.

Mr. Fairmount crouched over me, and I could feel his breath again on the back of my neck, in a whisper he asked, "Do you think he still loves you?"

I regarded his reflection in my mirror. What was it about John Fairmount that attracted so many people to him? He stood there before me, a god, expressionless, motionless.

I rose in defiance and turned to face him. But I found myself captivated by his presence. My heart beat faster. I stared into the dark abyss of his eyes. I took another step closer. I raised my hand to stroke his hair, and he grabbed my wrist, not once removing his gaze from mine.

"Mary," he said sternly.

Leaning in, while he held my wrist, I gently kissed his lips. They were so soft. I could feel his warm breath on my skin. I felt a small charge enter my body—one I have not felt since.

Was this what Lois felt? Was this what Lois had that I did not?

"No, Mary," he said, releasing my wrist.

My heart beat even faster. I was not deterred. A demon had possessed me. I was resolute. I took one more step closer.

"Mary," he said again. "Do not start something you will regret."

Another stalemate.

I reached up to stroke his hair, and this time, he did not grab my wrist. His hair was so soft, like mink. I felt a peculiar tingling sensation on my skin. I stood there transfixed. Mesmerized by the sensation. Powerless against my desires. It came in small waves; as soon as one ceased, another would take its place. Another yearning to be drawn into the abyss.

Lowering my hand by my side, I stared into his eyes, and an unusual calm followed. I felt my breathing start to labor. Rapid, short sessions as my chest rose and fell.

John Fairmount did not move. "Mary," he said calmly. "Think carefully. Some things cannot be undone."

I heard myself whisper, "Please."

"Are you asking this of me, Mary?" his voice was without emotion.

I whispered again, "Please."

"You know you need to say it out loud, Mary. You have to ask for what you want out loud. You have to claim your desires," he whispered in my ear. "What is it that you want?"

"I want what Lois has," I whispered back in his ear in desperation.

A smile passed across John Fairmount's lips, and, lifting his hand, he caressed the side of my cheek, and I was instantly paralyzed.

"If that is what you want, Mary . . ." he said, his voice trailing off.

He lifted my chin, and, leaning in, he kissed me passionately, and I was lost. Down into a deep chasm, I fell. I could not control my sensations. They were entirely at the whim and will of John Fairmount.

And when all had come to pass, as my heart pounded, he whispered in my ear, "I love you . . . Lois."

Those words broke whatever spell I had fallen under. The harsh reality of my actions came swirling into the room, as John Fairmount straightened his attire and left. I turned to my side and wept.

Chapter 18

It was Harry who rescued me, the day I ran into the woods, down the marble steps of Huntington House and out into the dense forest that surrounded it. I only wished to be engulfed by the trees and disappear. I wanted so desperately to disappear. Up until that moment, when Harry followed me, I did not really know if he loved me or not.

I can only explain my escape to the woods as a compulsion when I saw Harry again unannounced in Lois's room, leaning over, as I opened the door. The words entered my mind: *I want what Lois has.*

I could not take the madness. The madness of what I had done. The madness of jealousy that had so fervently taken hold of my heart now. The madness of being in awe and repelled by Lois Fairmount and enslaved by the whims and passions of John Fairmount.

I ran down the hallway, down the spiral staircase, out the heavy iron door, down the marble steps, across the gravel carriage-way, and through a dark canopy of trees, farther and farther way from Huntington House. I felt the cold air twisting around my lungs and the sting of vines tearing into my flesh, my mind possessed by the voices of those I harmed.

He caught me there in those woods. Leaping forward, Harry forced me to the ground, holding my shoulders down, his face pained. I would see the look of pain again sooner than I ever desired.

"I'd let you go, but you'd run away again," he said in between gasps of air. "This was a foolish thing to do, Mary. There are wild beasts in the woods. You could be hurt."

"I am hurt!" I cried.

He released his hold, sitting up. "I just wanted you to stop running," he said with a subtle sadness in his voice. "How are you hurt?"

"You!" I gasped. "You broke my heart! You don't love me. You only love Lois. Everyone loves Lois. Everyone always chooses Lois."

He laughed then. Not in cruelty but in amusement. Grabbing his arm, I rose.

"You are foolish! You ran all this way because I love Lois? I have never denied that." And, steadying my shoulders, he continued, "I love Lois. I love Lois because she is my only family in the world. I love Lois because I've known her my entire life. I love Lois because she knows my deepest, darkest secrets and will always keep them. I love Lois with every fiber of my being and always will."

I shook my head. I did not want to hear these words. These overwhelming words of devotion to Lois, pounding themselves into my soul. He loved Lois and not me. He would always only love Lois. John Fairmount was right. Harry would still come to Huntington House whether I was there or not. I was always the afterthought.

"There's no room for anyone else. You have no room for anyone else in your heart, Harry LaCroix. There is only Lois.

There is no room for me. No room for any woman besides Lois," I concluded sadly.

Releasing me, he laughed. "Mary Whitcombe, you are jealous of my aunt! You are jealous!" He studied me then, incredulously.

"You are afraid that because of my *familial* feelings of love and admiration for my *Aunt* Lois—the very aunt who is married to the dashing and wealthy John Fairmount, with whom I am told every woman in the world is in love, and is currently expecting *his* child, I might add—because of these feelings there is no room for another woman in my life. Am I understanding that properly?"

The animosity I had felt all this time, the acrimony that compelled me toward John Fairmount, that malevolence came forth as I screamed, "Yes! I have told you of my affections for you, Harry LaCroix. I have kissed you and pined for you and waited for you every weekend to come here to spend time with *me*. And all I do is find you've scurried off to your aunt's room!"

I continued, "I have taken countless walks with you in gardens and sat under trees and have done nothing to rebuff you, and yet you offer me nothing! There is nothing you have offered me, Harry. You don't come for me. You come for Lois."

And here he confessed—he confessed that he had spent too many years as a soldier in faraway places and had seen the horrors of war. That his soul was weary, and he buried himself in books and his work.

I could not listen any longer. I did not want to hear him. I did not want his words or his torments. I only knew mine. I knew how my heart broke so many times. I knew how my world had come crashing down so many times. I knew how any attempts at happiness were always taken far from me.

Soon, not even John Fairmount would have use for me. I failed with Harry.

"Mary," he finally said, "I live in a boardinghouse. I don't know what I have to offer you right now. I just have myself. But, in time, I may be able to offer you a cottage and that stream you talk so much about. I understand that you are frustrated, Mary. Those walks in the garden meant something to me. They meant something to me, Mary."

He started to remove twigs from my hair. "When I was a child, my mother and I lived off the charity of Aunt Lois and her mother. Drifters, really. Just the two of us." And here he breathed deeply. "My mother fell in love with a sailor when she was very young. He took advantage of her innocence."

My heart filled with guilt as he continued, "The only thing he left her was me—his bastard son." Those words came slowly and painfully to Harry. "I was judged harshly by everyone in the world but Lois. The world does not care for bastard sons regardless of how pure-hearted or intelligent they are. I've hidden that fact, and only you and Lois know."

I struck me then that Harry and I were the same. We both were hidden from the world. Neither of us would ever know our full parentage. Neither of us had a full place in the world. We were shadows. We were always hiding from ourselves and beholden to the kindness and generosity of others.

"I hope you come to understand, Mary, you have nothing to fear from Lois. I hope you will keep my secret now."

"I fear, Harry, that your confession may have come too late. I fear I have lost myself."

Harry smiled, that warm loving smile. "Mary, you are right here. You are not lost. You are with me." Holding my hands, he kissed them. "Come back with me now. It will be nightfall soon. Come back with me to Huntington House, will you?"

"And back to what?" I asked in a whisper. "Harry, I did not know about your past with Lois. Things have changed now . . . " An overwhelming sense of remorse washed over me. "You don't understand . . . I have betrayed . . . " but then the tears came flowing down my face.

"Is there something you need to tell me, Mary?" Harry asked, concerned. "Whatever it is Mary, I can forgive you." He smiled again, that lovely warm smile I hadn't seen in some time.

But what was I to say? How was I to confess? Where would I begin? How could I share the bargain that made me lose my soul?

I wiped the tears, and, breathing deeply, I said softly, "I can go back now."

Holding my hand, Harry LaCroix led me out of the darkness and back to Huntington House.

Chapter 19

It was shortly thereafter that John Fairmount found me in the library with my legs curled under me on the couch nearest the bookshelf. I had Shakespeare sonnets in my lap, reading Sonnet 35. This line I read over and over: "No more be grieved at that which thou hast done." It was my prayer for forgiveness. I read it over and over, as if Harry was reciting it to me.

"Mary," John Fairmount said, standing in the doorway. "A word?"

Rising, I followed him obediently to his study as I've always done. There was no sense that anything untoward had transpired between us in his demeanor. I questioned my own memory of the encounter. Perhaps it was a fancy I created because of my hatred. Perhaps it was a vivid dream and nothing more.

"Close the door, will you, Mary?" He stood behind his desk rifling through papers, and, holding up a brown envelope, he said, "The will, Mary. The very last piece arrived this morning, and, with it, your last task."

He placed the envelope gently on his desk. "I need you to convince my nephew to take an inheritance case he has declined."

I stepped forward, closer to the desk, my eyes fixed on the brown envelope. Within its confines was my freedom. "Why would he listen to me?"

"It is your future, Mary. I would have expected more enthusiasm. You came this far. It would be a shame to end all this now. Not this way, Mary. Not after all your efforts." His sharp tone made those last words sting.

"What would I say?" I asked stupidly. "How could I convince him?"

"I'm sure you'll find a way, Mary. You can be convincing when you're possessed," he said.

I swallowed hard.

"Why did you come here, Mary?" He tapped on the envelope, losing his patienc with me.

"My inheritance."

"And what do you want, Mary?" he asked directly.

"My freedom."

"And what secures that for you, Mary?"

"My fortune."

"With the will, Mary you are free to go," Mr. Fairmount continued, "and our agreement is concluded."

"What about Harry?" I asked, "Won't you need someone to keep him away from your wife?"

"No, Mary." he shook his head. "You've done that for me already."

"But he still visits her."

"Not for much longer. You'll secure that for me, too."

Placing his envelope in his desk drawer, he opened the door of his study, and I understood it was time for me to leave.

It was the next morning that I found Harry in the solarium. Mr. Gross had given me a fresh pot of tea to bring to
Harry. I regarded him, sitting there with his back turned. I
remember the shape of his head, and the gentle slump of his
shoulders. His chestnut hair was so perfectly placed. He wore
a white linen shirt, with a gray tailored vest of light wool.

I stood behind him. "Tea?"

Startled, he turned and smiled when he realized it was me.
"Mary! Yes, I would like some tea. I must not have slept at
all, since the women in this household seem to be prowling
around without my noticing and startling me." He offered
up his cup as I poured. "Normally I can note your perfume."

Having filled his cup, I placed the teapot on the serving
table and sat next to him.

"What kept you up so late, Harry? I'm sorry about my
outburst yesterday, with my running away as I did, and—"

"Think nothing of it. Who amongst us has not wanted
to run into a forest and be lost to the world? Are you done
with your concerns about my Aunt Lois?"

I nodded in agreement as Harry stirred his tea. "Why
did you not sleep?"

"Uncle John presented me with a case about some mine
claims. It seems that has become my calling now, since that
article in the paper."

"Is it about an inheritance?"

"Well, in part, yes. Good guess, Mary." He sipped his tea.

"You didn't want to do it for Mr. Fairmount?" I asked.

"Yes. I did not. I found it very interesting. I stayed up
the entire night reading through it all. By daylight, I had a
strategy." He placed his teacup on the table in front of him,
and, folding his arms, he squinted at the sun.

"And yet you declined?" I asked incredulously.

"Yes." He nodded.

I stood up, pacing now. "What if the case was incredibly important to a person's well-being? Was it the pay that made you decline? Were you not offered enough for taking on the effort?"

"They're just mines, Mary. Holes in Hades for the people who work them." Then he added, as if just considering it, "We didn't talk compensation. I declined."

"But what if you didn't decline? What if you asked for something that could secure our future?

"Mary, I . . . " he stuttered. "I would be gone a long time. I don't want to be gone from you and Lois."

"How long would be you gone?" I asked.

He shook his head unknowingly. "Christmas? It all depends on the case."

"What if I asked you to go?"

"Why would you ask me to go, Mary?" He chuckled.

"If your Uncle John paid you enough, we could buy that little cottage now as opposed to a year. We could . . . we could get married. We could leave here, and just start our own life. We could . . . "

"Why the sudden rush to get married?" He stood up and came toward me, rubbing my arms as if to soothe me. "We have plenty of time. I can do it on my own. I don't need Uncle John and his assignments."

Looking into my eyes, he smiled. "Surely you would miss me. You said yourself you've become quite accustomed to my comings and goings here at Huntington House." After kissing my forehead, he sat back down and closed his eyes.

"Why can't it be faster?" I asked in desperation. "Our marriage and our cottage. Why not sooner? Why do you always hesitate? Time is only for men."

He closed his eyes and settled into the bench.

I pleaded, "Harry, I want to have a family of my own. I want to have a roof over my head that is mine. Ours. I'm sorry if I am being so forward, but I am tired of being dependent on others for my security. First it was the convent, then the Longs, then the Fairmounts, and now I must wait on you? I want my own life. Mine! And only mine! I don't want to wait two years, or next Christmas. I am so very tired of being disappointed."

"What?" Harry asked, surprised and stirring awake. "Who has disappointed you?"

There was a silence that fell between us. I rose, stoic now. "I'm going to check on Lois. There's more tea in the pitcher. It seems you need it to stay awake."

And then, my last plea before leaving, "I urge you, Harry, to reconsider for all sakes."

Chapter 20

My pleading proved fruitful, as Harry accepted John Fairmount's assignment to secure mines. In exchange, Harry was granted a small parcel of land on the outskirts of Huntington House. It was a charming piece of property with a lovely stream flowing through, and nearby orchards. It was there we envisioned a small bridge where our children would play. It was far enough away so that any visit would need to be planned, and still close enough so Harry could be near to Lois and his nephew when he was born.

At first, I thought perhaps it was the emptiness I felt from Harry's departure that made me feel ill. I considered it an odd dispiriting that would pass when he returned. I was always tired. My mind would wander. My hands would inexplicably move to my middle. I did not for one moment believe that my indiscretion might have brought this forth. But as the weeks passed, I noticed a change in my appearance, and the very real possibility I was with a child—John Fairmount's child.

"Mr. Fairmount." I knocked on his study door.

"Come, Mary," he said, his hand leaning on his forehead. He was absorbed in some papers.

"May I close the door, Mr. Fairmount?" I asked.

Not looking up at me, he waved his hand in agreement. "Mary, were you an only child or did you have a sister?" he asked, still studying his papers.

"Mr. Fairmount," I started. "Mr. Fairmount, I need to talk with you."

Annoyed now, he looked up at me.

Looking down at my feet and twisting my fingers, I said quickly, "Mr. Fairmount, I think I might be with child."

He paused, looked up at me and then back down to his papers. "Well, then you should congratulate Harry on his return."

"But, Mr. Fairmount, I think that time. . ."

He raised his hand to silence me, and then, looking up, he said, slowly emphasizing each word, "Well, then, you should congratulate Harry on his return." Looking back down at his papers, he asked, "Is that all?"

"Yes," I said, bewildered.

"Then please leave the door open on your way out."

I walked up the staircase, slowly holding on to the railing. How was I going to congratulate Harry? We had never . . . Harry had always been a gentleman, restrained.

The weight of it all started to bear down on my shoulders. I was not forgiven. I was condemned.

When I reached the top of the staircase, Mrs. Fairmount opened her door. "Mary?" she asked.

I hurried up the remaining steps. "Mrs. Fairmount, you shouldn't be standing."

"Oh, please, Mary, don't start. I'm bored. See if you can find us a deck of cards, and let's play a hand."

Procuring a deck from her nightstand, I settled into a chair by Lois's bed.

"Pull that cart over and let's play here." As I dragged the emptied cart, she added, "Let's play whist."

"We don't have enough players," I offered. "We need four."

"Battle then?" Lois divided the cards into two piles. "Let's see who has the upper hand." Her eyebrow rose to the challenge, and then she looked over her cards. "Are you well, Mary? You look pale."

"I'm fine, ma'am." She nodded and smiled.

The game proceeded with Lois winning hand after hand. I sat restlessly, watching. "How did you learn to play?" she asked.

"Mrs. Long and I played in the afternoons." It was the first time my mind wandered back to my time with the Longs. I placed my next card down slowly. Who had I become in such a short time? A harlot? A betrayer? An opportunist?

"Mary, you're not even trying. You clearly have no heart for this," she said as she won again.

"How did you come to marry Mr. Fairmount?" I asked.

She smiled broadly, "Well, of all the men who asked, he needed me the least."

"It wasn't because he was handsome, or wealthy, or powerful?"

"He had his own fortune," Lois said absently.

"Mr. Fairmount's fortune must be vast then," I concluded.

"Oh, it's considerable. But mine is easily double." Here, she looked up and smiled. "Does that shock you?"

Looking down, she studied the cards before us. "Mr. Fairmount is man of considerable means. His reach is far and wide. He has mines and his investments—like the foolish thing he sent Harry on—" Here she placed down a Queen of Hearts. "But what many don't realize is I could easily devour all of John Fairmount's holdings with a mere telegraph—this house, all of it. And, one day, I just might." And here she looked up and smiled again. "Oh, don't look horrified, Mary. I probably won't."

I swallowed hard. "Who manages your fortune?" I asked slowly.

"Well, I do, dear, of course. It's been a bit harder now in my current condition, but I oversee it all."

"How?"

"That, dear Mary, is the trick of it. And one day, I might tell you. You see, Mary—I learned early on watching my mother's and my sister's misfortune that I would never let a single soul manage my money other than me. I kept up with Father. He explained it all. I was bright enough," she now placed down a Jack of Clubs, "and I learned. He really had no choice but to teach me. No one was really trustworthy. I had no brother, and he had no son." Here, placing her last card, she won again.

Looking up at me, slightly annoyed, she asked me pointedly, "Are you letting me win?"

"No."

"Oh, dear, then you really are bad at this." And she smiled again.

I felt a dryness in my throat as I stared at the ethereal Lois Fairmount and started to clear it. "If I may have some water?" I asked.

Nodding, she pointed at the table with the water pitcher and glasses as she shuffled the cards. It was while I was pouring my water that I saw the letter. It was unmistakably Harry's hand. In all the weeks he had been away, he had never written to me. I had not received a word. Lois followed my eyes staring at the letter.

"One more game, Mary. Yes, I was surprised Harry took that adventure. I'm sure he's written to you; he's well. Probably written you more than me."

But he had not written to me. I hadn't heard a word since his departure. I was crestfallen. I returned and sat down.

"It is unlike Harry to have taken it on. So unlike his nature." She started to deal the cards between us. "He has never, until this point, ever changed his mind. I'm not sure what to make of it."

"Perhaps he just wanted to secure a future for us."

"Oh, Mary. If you're seeking a fortune, Harry is not the man. Not that he's not intelligent enough; he's just not ruthless enough. Harry is good."

Lois stared at her cards, studying them. "I suppose you are well suited, as I expect you are good too, Mary, growing up in a convent. What do you even know about the demons and devils that are amongst us?"

I felt the room spin. Lois continued, "Ah, people worry about upsetting John Fairmount, when they don't even know the borders I can cross, the people I can move, by simply asking them. Oh, yes, my reach is far wider and more powerful than John Fairmount's, and he knows it. He just likes to ignore it. Like most men when confronted with something they don't care for, he pretends it's not real. People should really worry about crossing me." Placing her last card down, she exclaimed, "Ah! I won again."

But by now, I felt an overwhelming sickness. A heat rose through to my head.

"Mary?" Lois asked, concerned. "Mary, are you alright?"

That was the last voice I heard as my body hit the floor.

Chapter 21

I awoke hours later with a doctor at the foot of my bed. He was tall and thin, with gray eyes behind wire-rimmed spectacles. His brown and white speckled hair was neatly combed. He had a friendly mouth with thin lips and rounded cheeks. He was not the doctor who had come to attend Mrs. Fairmount. He was entirely different in both look and demeanor.

"Miss Whitcombe, I am Doctor Pierce. I was summoned here by Mrs. Fairmount on account of your fainting in her room. With your permission, I would like to examine you."

I had never been examined by a doctor before. I was always of fairly decent health, and whatever ailments I suffered were managed among the sisters.

When he concluded he placed his stethoscope around his neck, pulled my chair from the vanity and sat next to my bed.

"Mary," he said, his hands clasped together as he leaned forward, "do you know you are with child?"

I froze. Tears streamed down my face. Dr. Pierce looked down on the floor, and gently asked, "Does the young man know?"

I shook my head. He nodded knowingly.

"I think, Mary," he said again gently, "I would encourage you to inform the young man and marry swiftly. In short order Mary, dear, this will cease to be an option for you." He had the most sympathetic look on his face. He was downcast. He reached out and held my hand. After a while, he stood up and began to gather his things.

"Does Mrs. Fairmount know?"

He nodded. "But knowing Mrs. Fairmount, she would not dismiss you whether the young man married you or not. Please rest, Mary. Drink plenty of liquids and eat well." Turning the handle slowly, he left my room.

I lay there paralyzed. My sin now was fully exposed. My folly in bargaining for worldly goods. I was a lamb who joyfully danced to her own slaughter.

I pulled the curtain past the long window in my room and looked out into the solarium. The very solarium that John Fairmount pointed out during my arrival. Perhaps if I'd had more gratitude towards the Longs. Perhaps if I possessed less self-loathing, insecurity, and grief.

On my desk was the last puzzle piece for my fortune. A large brown envelope with a handwritten note placed gently on top of it, by Mr. Fairmount's hand —

Mary,
The will as promised. You are free to go. Our business is concluded.

John

And there I was. Dismissed. A betrayer to both Harry and Mrs. Fairmount, I leaned against the glass contemplating my future. My hand caressing the window latch. How far would be the fall? A gentle rapping at the door distracted me from my considerations.

The door swung open slowly, and there I saw Mr. Fairmount, with a woman on his arm.

"There you are, Mary!" he said cheerfully. "I have my last surprise for you." Here he smiled broadly.

"I fear, Mr. Fairmount, that I don't have the constitution for any more surprises. I read your note, and I will pack my things presently."

"Mary, please sit down," he said as one might instruct a child.

And like a well-trained child, I obeyed, sitting on the edge of my bed. He led the woman carefully and placed her in front of me. She was expressionless, thin and pale. She moved like an automaton. I wondered if her chest ever rose to take in air.

"Tell me, Mary. Does this woman here look familiar to you? Look at her face. Study her."

"Mr. Fairmount, I have no desire to play any more of your games." Looking at the woman in the green houndstooth suit, I addressed her, "I fear you may be playing part in a game in which you did not know you enlisted."

Here, her face brightened, and a tear fell down her cheek. She sang a tune I had long forgotten, so very long ago, it echoed in the back of my brain.

Hush, my dear one,
Sleep serenely,
Now, my lovely
Slumber deep.
Mother rocks you,
Humming lowly,
Close your eyes now
Go to sleep

"How do you know that song?" I asked, weeping. "My mother sang me that song." Angrily, I turned to Mr. Fairmount. "Is this another one of your tricks? One of your pawns you drudged up from some desperate hovel? Haven't you done enough, Mr. Fairmount?"

But Mr. Fairmount leaned on my bureau by the door, lit his cigarette and smiled. And then, resting his elbow on his arm, he blew three rings. "Do you remember when I asked you if you were an only child?" Urging the woman, he said, "Perhaps you'd like to tell Mary who you are."

And then the automaton spoke, "Mary. Mary, do you remember when you were little? We played. You had a table with teacups and dolls. Remember you would hold my hand and steady me down the stairs while our nanny complained about the loud thudding of my shoes. Do you remember me, Mary? Do you remember me?"

Here she raised her hands to wipe the tears that flowed uncontrollably from her eyes. "Do you remember me? My name is Fiona. Tell me that name means something to you, and you were not too little to remember me." She broke down uncontrollably and wept, and I rose, putting my arms around her and, steading her, I guided her to the bed next to me. I held her. Her thin frame shook on my shoulder as he gasped for air and wept.

"My dear woman," I said, stroking her hair, "I don't know what Mr. Fairmount has told you, but my sister died with my parents at sea."

"No!" She pulled away from my grasp. "No. No. She did not die. I am *her*. When Mama and Papa were to leave, I started to run a fever. They did not take me. I was left behind as you. But I was ill and weak, and I could not come to you, Mary. And you, you did not know I was there, did you? And then Thomas, Uncle Thomas took me in. The convent would not take me because of my eyes."

Then, reaching into a deep pocket in the green hound-stooth dress, she pulled out the smallest, most delicate porcelain teacup with a gold rim and pink painted roses. "I kept this for you. It's your teacup. Do you remember them? You used to always leave your stuffed rabbit and dolls to watch over them when we went out outside to play."

I held it in my hand, turning it over. All the memories assaulted my mind. The sounds of Fiona and I playing outside. The sunlight coming through my bedroom window and onto my table with all my teacups. The sounds of Fiona giggling as we pretended to pour our tea.

"I, I can't." I rose quickly and noticed that Mr. Fairmount was no longer in the room. "This is just another trick of Mr. Fairmount's."

"Mary. Mary, I know this is hard, but I am her. How can I prove it? Do you remember that scar you have on the back of your left knee? It was my fault. I pushed you too hard on the swing, and you fell on that stone. Do you remember? How would Mr. Fairmount know of that scar?"

I put my hand over my face. After a pause, I said, "I would love nothing more at this moment than to have family. You have no idea how lonely it's been. Why didn't you find me before? *If it is you!*"

"I could not reach you when I was little. And no pleas to Uncle Thomas would persuade him to bring me. I wrote the convent letters. Reaching into her pocket again, she brought forth a stack of wrinkled, tear-stained letters tied in a yellow ribbon and handed them to me. "They were always returned unopened. I thought it meant you perished. They kept us apart to protect us, Mary. There would have been many try-ing to control our fortune, and Uncle Thomas, for his part, kept as much of it whole as he could. But there was a man who came to see him. Harry . . . a Harry LaCroix, who said he knew you, and he was there on your behalf. And Uncle Thomas told him to bring you to him, and he would have the will. But he never returned, and he never returned with you."

Twisting my fingers together, I said, "I asked him to stop. Not to continue seeking my fortune."

"He did know you then! I loved the sound of his voice. Is he your solicitor?"

"No. He's a friend. He's a solicitor. But he is a friend to me, I suppose."

We spoke there for hours, Fiona and I. Small pieces of memories of our home and childhood. The more she spoke, the more I remembered. All those beautiful, sweet memories tucked away. I was not alone in the world. I was never alone in the world. Somewhere another heart beat like mine.

Mr. Gross came to get her and let us know her carriage had arrived. Walking down the stairs with her, we made arrangements for our next meeting and my departure from Huntington House. It was then, waving from the front door, that I heard Lois Fairmount's voice emanating from Mr. Fairmount's study. I approached and looked through the crack of the door. John Fairmount was seated facing Mrs. Fairmount.

"Any news of Harry?" she asked.

"Lois, darling, why do you insist on coming down the stairs?"

"Harry, John. What news?"

He leaned back in his chair and placed his hands behind his head, "Your nephew, is a genius, my dear Lois. He secured the mines. He won his case."

"You don't need to flatter me about Harry." Lifting a pen from his desk and turning her back to him as she twisted it with her fingers, she asked, "Nothing more? Nothing more to tell me, John?"

A frigid silence fell.

"He should be arriving imminently," John Fairmount offered, unnerved by his wife.

She nodded slowly, placed the pen back on his desk, and turned to leave. "You know that Mary isn't feeling well." Her back was still turned to him.

"I heard."

She nodded. "Yes. I fetched a doctor for her," Mrs. Fairmount said.

"I'm glad Mr. Gross could assist," he said.

"No, John. This is a doctor *I* fetched for Mary."

Another silence fell, and Mr. Fairmount leaned back in his large leather chair, studying his wife. She stood there. A glowing, solid, marble-like figure with her back to him. I held my breath. Slowly, Mrs. Fairmount turned and walked gracefully to the door.

But before she reached the door handle, she said, "Would you like to tell Harry when he arrives that the child Mary is carrying is yours, or shall I?"

She did not await a reply but slowly walked into the solarium.

Chapter 22

It was the banging of the brass knob on the large wooden doors to Huntington House that announced Harry's arrival. I spent the day gathering my belongings. I had hoped to spare Harry the pain of it all and disappear, but he arrived faster than anyone anticipated. I crouched on the top step and listened. I heard him drop his bags on the floor. No one came to greet him, as was always done prior.

"What the devil is wrong with this place?" he whispered. "It's a mausoleum."

I heard his steps toward the solarium. I knew Lois was there. I went into my room and looked through the window to the solarium. I could see Lois seated on a bench. And Harry, smiling broadly, until he wasn't. He leaned down and held her hand, and then, releasing it, stood violently.

She stood with him. They spoke. With his back to my view and covering her silhouette, I could tell no more, other than his violent pace out the door.

A terror then gripped my heart. I sat, still on the edge of my bed, staring at the floor and biting my lower lip. In time

I heard his hard rapid footsteps as he raced up to my room. He swung my bedroom door open with a tremendous force, and I recoiled. I never knew Harry to be so violent. He was always gentle and careful. But there he was wild. My eyes fixed on the floor, fearful.

"How could you?" he yelled. "With my uncle John? While I was away, Mary? While I was away doing his bidding so I could satisfy you and build our future, as you asked . . ." Words faltered. "Why did you do it, Mary? Did he force himself upon you?"

"No. Never," I said, still twisting the handkerchief between my fingers and keeping my voice low and careful so not to incite him any further. "It's not what you think."

He furiously bellowed, "Answer me this. Are you with child? Are you with *John's* child?"

Out of fear, I did not answer the question, knowing full well the injustice I had perpetrated toward his affections. "I have a sister," I said, still not raising my gaze to look at him. "Her name is Fiona. She's alive. She was never on the ship. She was left behind, like me, and I did not know. She was living with a lawyer all this time, a former family friend who used to oversee my father's affairs. Mr. Fairmount found her for me while you were away. He brought her here for us to meet." I stared at the floor, not moving. And for the moment, Harry stopped pacing about the room like a caged lion.

"She has a condition," I continued. "It's her eyes. The convent wouldn't take her, so they separated us. The lawyer separated us." Gulping down hard, I steadied my voice. "I met her. I met my sister. Mr. Fairmount arranged it. She's visited me here," I repeated.

He quieted.

I rose and hurriedly ran across the room. Opening a drawer from the chest, I retrieved a large envelope. "It is a record of my birth and hers. It shows that we are Whitcombes. Both she and I are Whitcombes."

I gasped for air as emotions overtook me, staring down at the envelope in my hands. I knew full well what I had done to secure that brown, tear-stained envelope. "The lawyer, Payne, kept it in a hidden safe, telling her all these years that all was lost. She thought I had died. But a man came to inquire after my father's will. Fiona heard them talk. Was that you, Harry? Did you find Thomas Payne?"

I went back to my bed and sat. I placed the papers to my right. Harry was calmer now. I whispered, "I lived alone in the stone walls of the convent when I could have been together with my sister. I could have been with my family. I have a sister. Mr. Fairmount found my sister and brought her to me."

"And for these papers, you gave yourself to him? Was this your form of payment?" he yelled again, anger renewed.

"No. It was an act of gratitude, and nothing more," I whispered. How could I tell him it was jealousy coupled with insecurity.

He scoffed. "Gratitude?" He nodded. "Yes. Indeed. What else but gratitude? What else did you have to give in return besides yourself?"

He stood still. Time stood still.

"I do not love him," I said.

"Who do you love, then?" he asked mockingly.

"You."

He stared at the celing and closed his eyes.

"I found your letter to Lois. It was buried under her books." I began to wipe tears from my face. It would be me and Fiona now, and my child. There was no need to be apologetic anymore. "In all the time you were gone, you never wrote me."

"I had your portrait on my dresser. Not Lois's, for God's sake. It was *yours*!" Harry replied, enraged again.

"I did not mean for this to happen." And for the first time, I looked up at him, and, seeing his face, I remarked, "Your face! You have blood on your face!"

"The child is John's?" he asked in a cold tone, turning to face me.

I nodded. It did not matter now.

"And no other?"

I nodded again and burst into tears. "What in the world did I do?" I mumbled, more to myself than anyone else, and, putting my hands over my face, I sobbed. "I don't know what possessed me. I did not intend for this to happen at all."

Harry paced my room again while I wept bitterly. It was done now. All of it was done. My selfishness. My pettiness. My failure. All done. Wiped away from this moment on. Fiona and I would claim our fortune. We would return to those iron gates as John Fairmount promised. And I, as the final pawn, would have put a permanent wedge between Harry and Lois. I cried to purge myself. To let it all go.

But to my surprise, Harry pulled my hands from my face and kneeled before me. "Mary," he said calmly now, in the tone he always addressed me with before that day and ever since, "Mary, look at me." I stared into his lovely eyes those eyes that have always brought me peace. "Mary, are you certain that you love me? Do you truly love *me*?"

"Yes. I love you, and only you," I said, my voice breaking.

He grabbed my hands. "Mary, how far along are you with this child?"

"A few weeks," I said.

"Mary, would you consent to me raising the child as my own? We can be married in a few day's time, and we'll say it was mine, and that the child came early. No one needs to know it is not my own flesh and blood."

"But Mr. and Mrs. Fairmount know . . ."

"I'm quite certain I could convince them to not share it with a soul," he said soothingly. "Does anyone else know, Mary, that you are with child? This is important. Does anyone else know the child belongs to John besides Lois, John, you, and me?"

"No," I whispered.

"Not the doctor? Not Fiona? No one?" he asked again

"No. No one else."

Letting go of my hands, he rose again and paced the room once more.

I looked about my room and remembered the joy when I first saw it. The happiness it brought. The time and attention Mr. Fairmount paid to ensure it was well appointed and beautiful.

Harry knelt before me. "Marry me, Mary. Let me care for the child. I will love the child as an innocent with all my heart for all my days. No one will ever need to know it is not mine." And, saying so, he placed an emerald ring on my finger. I stared in disbelief.

"Mary," he continued as one might speak to a child, "Mary, I know you have been broken. But I vow to you, with all my heart, that I will spend the rest of my life trying to heal you. Will you?" he asked intently. "Will you marry me?"

"Yes!" I exclaimed. "Yes, I will marry you."

"Then let us leave. Let us leave this moment. Now, Mary! Let us never look back. Let us mark this moment as the beginning of all things new. You as a new Mary. And I as a new Harry."

I nodded and embracing me, he held me close. We ran down the mahogany stairs for the last time.

Swinging the doors open and running down the marble steps, he yelled, "Gross! Gross, damn you. I know you are near! I know you are near like all demons to their *master!* The motor coach, Gross!" He released my hand. "Fetch me your master's motor coach!"

As he turned his head to face the circular driveway, as if it was predetermined, the automobile appeared. Harry entered it, slamming the door and shouting back, "You can tell Mr. Fairmount this is also part of my payment."

I can still hear the sound of the wheels on the gravel as we left. The final sound of my freedom. And the beginning of my life as Mary LaCroix. No longer chained as a Whitcombe. No longer beholden to a Fairmount.

Epilogue

The ceremony was held in a small chapel on the outskirts of town that neither Harry nor I had ever attended, but the vicar was an elderly gentleman who asked very few questions and was just pleased with his stipend. I wore an ivory lace dress with tiny pink embroidered roses. It was a gift couriered over by Lois Fairmount, with a small card, along with all the documents I had left behind. On the card, she wrote:

Mary—
Make Harry happy.
—L

In my hands, I held a small bouquet of wild white daisies, and Harry wore his gray suit with a pink rose in his lapel. In attendance were Fiona and Harry's friend, Joseph, who had previously presided over the case with the mines for Mr. Fairmount during Harry's absence. Joseph has become a close confidant in all our years and serves as godfather to all our children.

Harry and I settled into a small apartment above the hotel near his work at the Solicitor General's Office, and I spent my time staring out windows and sitting in chairs waiting for the baby to come. It was on one such occasion when I received a post. It was a large envelope from Lady Isabella. I held it in my hand, contemplating the contents, turning it over slowly several times and, watching the light of the window cast shadows. Cautiously, I opened it. A small letter fell out, and it read as follows:

My Dearest Mary,

I heard of your recent nuptials and send my heartfelt best wishes. I understand it was a very small affair, and I harbor no dark sentiments for the lack of invitation, as I'm sure you expected me to be in mourning with Frederick's sudden passing. I hope that nephew of Lois Fairmount is made of better character than her choice of husband. Why a woman would marry a man like John Fairmount is beyond my comprehension.

Frederick's death came as quite a shock, and I hope you do not judge him harshly, for he always had the best intentions for you as your godfather. He did not want to tell you immediately, hoping you would come to feel warmly towards him as one might any father figure. Your sudden departure struck him very hard and brought him back to your disappearance as a child.

He had not known of your whereabouts, thinking that perhaps only Fiona was left behind and you had gone with your parents on that ship. He thought perhaps there had been some confusion with the children. He came to claim you as soon as he saw the advertisement in the paper for your art, and I will say, he was not pleased that you had been hidden for so long.

Know that he loved your father dearly. He hoped also in time, you would come accustomed to high society since no doubt you were not used to unsavory, dishonest, and manipulative characters in the world having spent so much of your life behind the safe walls of the convent.

By now you must know that you are the owner of several mines. Frederick tried hard to secure what he could for you. Enclosed you will find your father's last will and testament, which he had entrusted to Frederick. There have been many throughout the years who hoped to find it, sometimes threatening Frederick, even as far off as Italy, if you could possibly imagine! Nonetheless, I hope it serves you well. There is no point in my keeping it any longer.

For my part, I will be closing the manor house and setting off to travel the world again. My heart is heavy with the loss of Frederick. He was a good man and a good husband. I will look for solace in the world and in art.

Take good care, Mary. Remember there are those who do evil in the world, but always keep in your mind, they can do you no harm unless invited.

Your godmother,
Lady Isabella Long

Acknowledgments

I am forever grateful to my incredible friend, Jami Birnbaum, who continues to read every single draft of anything I write. She is unequivocably kind, gracious, and generous with her time. A sincere thank you to Jane Ubell-Meyer, Robert Robinson, and Doreen Marchetti, whose unwavering support always keeps me going when I doubt myself. And finally, a massive thank you to Krista Venero who suffered through my grammar and my love of em dashes.

To my amazing sons: remember that anything is possible, even your mother writing books at her age.

Keep reading for a sneak peek at
The Fairmounts Book Three:

Abigail Fairmount

Chapter 1

It is a strange thing to live a lie. It's never a thing that a reasonable person decides to be the direction of his life. It is often an emotional response, a moment of extreme weakness or discomfort. It is a thing of paramount regret, however noble the cause, and as such, it has been with me.

Anyone who has led a life of deception will tell you that you start to settle into it over time. You start to forget it. You become this new half creation who can in many ways, carry on as if a decent personage with the appropriate level of righteousness. But your soul, ah, your soul is aware. It knows that you have sacrificed a portion of yourself, a portion of your ultimate goodness, so that this lie, this tiny little deceit can in some ways conceal the circumstance of its arrival.

My lie. My deep deception. That thing which I regretted each time I looked into my darling little Abigail's eyes. Every time, she held her hands up to me with her dark curls flowing and called me, "Papa, Papa, pick me up and swing me round!"

Oh, I hear her giggle, that angelic giggle as I held her tighter and loved her with every inch of my being, my beautiful, darling little girl, Abigail. I could convince myself to believe it then, at those moments, that she was unequivocally mine.

And then it would come. Those moments of reminder. Those moments when I could hear Abigail's little voice when she addressed her Uncle John at gatherings. John, always impeccably dressed, unshakeable, cigarette in one hand while holding Abigail's hand in the other, walking through the rose garden, or on his knees, serving as her wayward stallion, galloping about. Her voice carried to me, on the wind, "I wish Papa was as brave as you Uncle John, and my father was in the Africa Wars!" And other times, "Oh, tell me another story of your adventures Uncle John! Papa never tells me stories."

They were always inseparable when they came to be into each other's company.

But to understand my heartbreak, I would need to take you to the beginning, to the very moment, when I absorbed a lie, that I knew in my heart would forever banish me from my own thoughts of honor, for it was not a lie that suited me. It was a lie manifested at the disadvantage of so many others. It was the hiding of truth of which I had acquired ownership and would not release. It would forever condemn me to live a life of torment, of pained existence. To understand it, I must take you to the moments that followed as I ran down the grand staircase of Huntington House, with Mary Whitcombe being dragged behind me. Yes, that moment when I traded my soul for John Fairmount, for the salvation of Mary's and the disillusion of Abigail's. It is there that I must begin.

"Mr. Gross!" I yelled at the top of my lungs on the bottom steps of Huntington House, the Greek marble revival that was the home of my Aunt Lois and John Fairmount. That house where just moments before, I had betrothed Mary Whitcombe. Mary had served as a nanny for my aunt and was the forgotten heiress to the Whitcombe fortune. I held Mary's hand tightly in mine. "Where the devil are you, Gross? I know you can hear me!"

How did it come to this? My shouting as a lunatic outdoors, with no regard to any sense of propriety for my aunt's home. My beautiful Aunt Lois, who was but a mere seven years older than I. She was always my champion, my confidant, my protector. But there, in Huntington House, it was clear to me now, it was Mephistopheles who ruled, and Lois, my dear, angelic Lois, was to serve as the only light, the only uncorruptible in the salvation of John Fairmount's soul. A bargain she had made with John so very long ago, in which I was now ensnared.

I released Mary's hand and walked onto the gravel. I waved my hat. "I want the motor car! John Fairmount's glorious, precious motor car!"

I walked in a circle like a madman, running my fingers in my hair. "Not the horse and carriage, Gross!" I could feel the cold air encircling me, "Oh sod it!" Turning swiftly, I found Mary shivering on the stairs. "Don't move. I'll be back."

Jogging to where John kept his motor cars, I found one running with a blanket in place and I knew. I knew John had foreseen it all, orchestrated it all, used Lois's nature against mine. He wanted me to marry Mary Whitcombe. He wanted me to have her secret be mine forever more. His perpetual and permanent gift to me for my nature which up until then, was to avoid dishonesty, greed, and avarice. My seeking of Mary's fortune was simply to provide her with a freedom to choose. A freedom to cast aside the poverty she knew as the orphan in the convent. A freedom to be her own master. A freedom that I, myself, did not have as the forgotten bastard son of a sailor, who hid his shame under the shroud of service and schooling.

I jumped into the motor car and drove to the front of Huntington House. I found Mary, sitting on the marble steps a huddled mass, shivering. I helped her into the automobile, sitting her by my side, and clasping her cold hands. I wrapped the blanket left for us around her shoulders. In my most reassuring voice I could offered, "We'll be fine, Mary." Putting the motor car into gear, I said, half under my breath, "You'll never have to come here again."

The sun began to set by the time we arrived in the city. My passionate escape did not have either of us well prepared, and I knew that with Mary's nature, she would by now be worried. I pulled into an inn, near where I was employed at the Solicitor General's Office, and after helping Mary out of the vehicle, entered with her and rang the bell.

An older stoic woman came to the front desk. "Can I help you, sir?"

"Yes," I said while Mary shivered. "Yes. I would like to secure a room for my betrothed." Lifting Mary's hand, I showed the woman, the emerald ring, I had given Mary hours prior. The emerald ring my mother left me, before her passing. The ring that Lois held for me all these years, while I was at war. My last memento of my mother.

"She is not from here," I said carefully. "and I am merely a bachelor with lodging down the way. So, until we have it all sorted, my . . . Mary, will need lodging. I heard great things about your establishment."

"Well," she said sternly, straightening her bodice, "we only house women. And fortunate for you, I do have one apartment left, which I will let to you, for thirteen shilling a week, starting at this moment."

"Thank you." I handed her a pound, which I saw caused considerable surprise. "Please make sure there is a fire for her, and supper."

Now turning to Mary, I said, "I have arrangements I need to sort. Please eat something. You've had enough of a shock for today. Just know that I love you, and I will return." After kissing her on the cheek, I left Mary, wrapped in a blanket, uncertain about either of our futures.

I drove to my own abode, my place of lodging where my shirts were ironed, my meals served, and my room tidied. I had no wants in the world there, and I could lose myself in my books, in my work, in my own imagination.

I unlocked my door and lit the gas lantern. Removing my tie, and throwing my jacket on the wooden chair, I looked about it all. There, on the desk, were the papers I had read last before I left for my, the adventure where I was enlisted by John Fairmount, to secure his claims on a mine that unknown to me at the time, was rightfully Mary's. I placed my pocket watch next to the pile of papers.

Sitting on the edge of my bed, I removed my shoes, one by one, and reflected on the brilliance of John Fairmount's ploy. That in exchange for a parcel of land, so that Mary and I could build our home and start our future, I would argue on John's behalf, and beat his enemies. Oh, the foolish joy, I felt during my return. My jubilation to share with Mary that she was now a mine owner, that my Uncle John Fairmount had gifted it to us. There on the nightstand were the architectural drawings I commissioned before I left. The drawings for a house I had so painstakingly imagined for both of us, with no detail left undiscovered. I even imagined a room for Mary to paint whatever her heart desired and asked the architect to place it where the sun would shine the longest and the purest.

I fell back on my bed. My hands clasped over my face. In the morning, I would need to find a small church and make the arrangements to marry Mary. I would need to collect Mary's things. I would need to return the motor car.

I stared at the ceiling. I would need a new life now. Another iteration of myself would be required. My dream of Lois and I being together, free like when we were children was shattered. I was soon to be a father to a child not my own, and a husband to a wife who had doubted my fidelity. I turned my head and looked out the window as the sun cast its final rays and the last of its shadows. Tomorrow, my new life would begin.

Chapter 2

I awoke late the next morning, dressed and shaved. I remember my reflection as I touched my face to ensure I had cleaned up appropriately. *There you are, Old Chap.* I thought to myself, *You are now to be a good husband and a good father. On this and this alone, the Lord will judge you. Step onto solid ground, Old Chap. From this moment on, your life will not be your own.*

I decided that my first duty was to secure a marriage license, which would require a trip to the town hall and then to the courthouse. The idea of it all seemed so overwhelming. John had already secured a generous leave for me from the Solicitor's General's Office to argue on his behalf, and I was not expected to return for another week. It was here that Providence stepped in and delivered to me, a man who was to become my greatest friend and godfather to all my children. It was as I opened the door that I stood face to face with Joseph, the magistrate who presided over the property dispute with the mines not a short time past. His arm was in midair ready to knock on the door, and I dare say, opening it so unexpectedly as I did, I gave us both a fright.

"Mr. LaCroix, Harry," he said catching his breath, "I didn't mean to startle you. I was coming through this way, and I thought I would hand deliver my judgement to you regarding the mines, personal delivery as it were."

I was overjoyed to see him. Joseph, short of statue, but profound of heart. "Would you, want to eat something with me?" I fumbled for the words as I took the large envelope from his hand. "There is a small pub, nearby. As a thank you for your trouble and travels."

Joseph's blue eyes sparkled, he hopped slightly as he said with the utmost delight, "I am famished."

We settled ourselves at the same table I sat with Mary less than a year ago, on our very first meeting, appointed with a lovely white linen tablecloth. We both ordered sandwiches and ale, and after a small silence, Joseph, licking his fingers inquired, "Whatever happened to the baby? Are you an uncle?"

"No," I replied with what Joseph must have regarded as the saddest sigh, as he stopped licking his fingers and stared at me in the pause of time, before anything horrific was uttered, "She's still waiting for my nephew's arrival, I . . . "

Here I could not continue. I looked down at my napkin and started to fold it over, "You see, Joseph, I am to be married, I think . . . "

"Well, you wouldn't know it, by the look of you, just now! You'd think someone had died. If you're not overjoyed, why in the world are you getting married? It seems to me that such things cannot be entered into lightly. It's a lifetime, my dear man."

Nodding, I explained, "I am marrying to save the young woman, as much as myself and my aunt."

Joseph cocked his head to one side and knitted his brows, as I continued, "but it seems to me that it was John Fairmount who had the better of us all."

"John Fairmount, the man you represented who is married to your aunt?" he inquired unemotionally. I nodded. "And who pray tell are you marrying?"

"Mary Whitcombe."

Here, Joseph could not help by laugh. And laugh he did the jolly man, so much so, that I laughed myself! After the both of us caught our breaths, Joseph, wide-smiled shook his head and said, "That is the most ridiculous thing I have heard. As a magistrate, I have heard quite some things."

"I stole a car, Joseph. I stole John Fairmount's car."

And here Joseph giggled, like old Saint Nicholas, with his arms around his belly and such delight.

"I suppose . . . I should . . . return it . . ." I said between bouts of laughter. By now all the patrons had stopped their meals and started squarely at the two lunatics by the window, who had keeled over with laughter, after only half a pint of ale.

My confession to Joseph, of all that transpired between Mary, myself, John Fairmount, and my aunt Lois, eventually sobered us both, and we sat staring out the window, as the horse drawn carriages and motor cars rolled by. The sun had risen higher in the sky now. The afternoon was now upon us.

"I will help you." Joseph said after a long silence, "I must ask first, do you love, Mary?"

"Yes," I said.

"Are you certain?"

"Yes."

"And you would have married her otherwise, regardless?"

"Yes. I had an architect draw plans for our cottage. I have the deed to the land that John granted me. It's just accelerated it all, I suppose."

"Well, I will help you, because it is by far the noblest and most self-less sacrifice, I have ever heard in all my years so far. I'm not quite sure any of them deserve it, but if you are resolute, I will help you."

"I am."

And before I could settle payment for our meals, Joseph, had already opened the door and motioned that I move quickly. By late afternoon, Joseph had secured our wedding license, and signed it himself, "I'll serve as your man as well" he said as we drove out to the country to a church Joseph was certain would marry us.

"You're quite organized," I shouted over the bumpy dirt road that jostled us about.

Holding his hat Joseph quipped, "I married three sisters in various stages of virtue. It's right up there to the left."

And here we rounded the corner from the trees and rambles and steered into a small courtyard of stone with a small wooden chapel, painted white with a lovely copper bell up on the high steeple which seemed extravagant and out of place. Around the stone walls were fragrant pink wild English roses that we coming to the season's end, and a faint scent of lavender that had dried on its stalks.

"Grab the bottle of rum we purchased and follow me," Joseph instructed.

Joseph stood on the small white wooden porch and held the iron knocker in this hand, tapping lightly. Then, he placed his hands in his pockets while he shifted his weight from the balls of his feet to the back of his heels as if in a bit of dance. Minutes passed with us standing in silence, but Joseph, not remotely concerned, waited patiently smiling.

In due time, the door opened, and a man with snow white hair, frail of statue, and only a foot taller than Joseph, answered the door. He was hunched slightly with white robes, embroidered with gold thread, underneath which he wore a white shirt and religious collar.

"Oh, Mr. Whyte!" he exclaimed when he saw him. Releasing Joseph from a warm embraced, he said in a low voice, "Tell me, do you have another sister to marry?" Then looking up and over at me, an expression of slight panic passed over his visage.

"No, thank goodness. They're all sorted now, I think. This is my friend, Harry LaCroix." I balanced the bottle of rum and extended my hand to shake the clergyman's. "He is going to marry a lovely woman, Mary forthwith, and needs a church and a preacher."

Seeing the bottle of rum in my hand, the expression on the minister's face widened, and he beckoned us in.

The inside of the church did not match its exterior. Inside, were beautiful marble statues of the Virgin Mary and other saints. The windows not visible from the front were all stained glass, with various depictions of the stages representing the passion of the cross. The floor was a remarkable solid stone, and the altar was most intricately carved from mahogany, with the light fixtures above encased in gold filigrees.

"This chapel was built about eighty years ago," the clergyman continued, "by an earl who wanted to marry his mistress. He built it so no one would know it was here, and made it appear the most modest, so no one would stop and question. He waited until the servants informed him his wife died, as she was ill and before the cock could crow twice, they were married right there." Here he stopped and pointed to a spot in front of the altar.

Straightening himself up ever so slightly as a point of pride, he continued, "It was my father who rightly married them. My family has overseen this church ever since." Turning to me he said very seriously, "We only do weddings here. And only the true love sort. Is yours true love?"

"Yes," I said.

Clearing his throat, Joseph nudged my arm to deliver to the clergyman his rum. He accepted it greedily and then turned back to stare at the altar and the large wooden crucifix with the wreathe over the Lord and Savior encrusted in gold.

"When would you like to have the holy ceremony?" the clergyman asked.

"Overmorrow at noon," Joseph answered for me.

Nodding his head and smiling, the clergyman tapped his bounty lightly and left us to find our own way out.

When we reached the motor car, Joseph beamed. "This is much more pleasant an experience when there's no familial attachments or weeping siblings."

Boarding the automobile while drumming his hand on the door once closed, he announced, "I think I would very much like to acquire one of these things. So, dear Harry, I think it's time to deliver this to the rightful owner before the constable comes looking for us both. Besides, I am fascinated to see Mr. Fairmount himself. He's a bit of a legend, you know?" turning to me and smiling again he said as one might address a horse, "Haya!" and shifting the gear, we were off.

About the Author

Valerie Nifora is an award winning and best-selling author of fiction, poetry and nonfiction. She was born and raised on Long Island to Greek immigrant parents. Her romance series The Fairmount was featured on NBC Los Angeles, California Live and Lux Lifestyle Magazine's Hot Book List (2022, 2023) among other publications. When not moonlighting as a writer and speaker, Valerie serves as Fortune 50 Global Marketing Leader. She is married and a mother to two amazing sons.

Learn more about Valerie and her works at www.valerienifora.com

Thank You

Thank you for choosing to read *Mary Whitcombe.*

If you enjoyed the book, would you please consider leaving a review online with the retailer of your choice? It would mean a lot to me.

Invite me to your book club!

Do you have a book club? I'd love to join your discussion virtually or in person. Just reach out! I'm also available for readings, signings, and speaking engagements.

Visit me at ValerieNifora.com

Join me on social

Please join wherever you are. I share glimpses into my life, work, and passions! Here's to all good things!

- 📷 : @valerienifora
- 𝐟 : @Valerie Nifora
- in : @vnifora

www.ValerieNifora.com

True Love. Heartbreak.
Deep Family Secrets.

"A beautiful romance novel, full of suspense,
mystery, tales of old legends and so much more."
— Theresa Kadair, *Seattle Book Review* ☆ ☆ ☆ ☆ ☆

Available on Amazon and other retailers.

We all seek love.

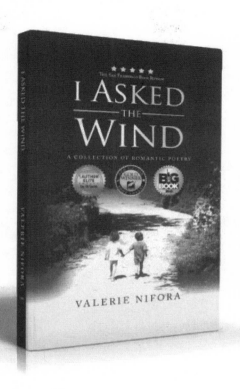

185

Made in the USA
Middletown, DE
24 February 2024

49624716R00118